DUPLIKATE

DUPLIKATE

A NOVEL BY CHERRY CHEVA

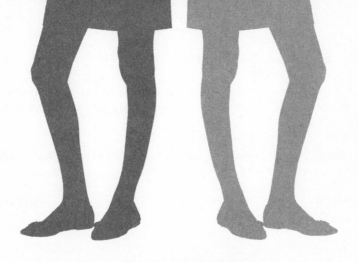

HARPER TEEN

An Imprint of HarperCollinsPublishers

Produced by Alloy Entertainment
151 West 26th Street, New York, NY 10001

Library of Congress Cataloging-in-Publication Data
Cheva, Cherry.
    DupliKate / by Cherry Cheva. — 1st ed.
       p.   cm.
    Summary: When she wakes up one morning to find her double in her room,
seventeen-year-old Kate, already at wit's end with college applications, finals, and extracurricular activities, decides to put her to work.
    ISBN 978-0-06-128854-8 (trade bdg.)
    [1. Computer games—Fiction.   2. Virtual reality—Fiction.   3. Identity—Fiction.
4. Interpersonal relations—Fiction.   5. Self-perception—Fiction.   6. High schools—Fiction.   7. Schools—Fiction.]   I. Title.
PZ7.C42556Du   2009   2009018292
[Fic]—dc22   CIP
                                                                  AC

Design by Andrea C. Uva

09 10 11 12 13 LP/RRDB 10 9 8 7 6 5 4 3 2 1

First Edition

FOR MY FAMILY

DUPLIKATE

CHAPTER ONE
SUNDAY, DECEMBER 2

"I HATE YOU," I TOLD MY BOYFRIEND.

After a long weekend of studying for finals, dealing with prom committee, going over the school paper layout, and starting page designs for the yearbook, I was sitting with Paul in the Starbucks next door to our high school.

"This is so awesome it makes me want to kill myself," I declared, waving his college application essay in the air. "Or at least tear my hair out." I slammed the neatly stapled sheets down onto the tabletop next to my peppermint mocha. I would have slammed my face down as well, but Paul's hand shot out in time to stop me. We froze for a second, his palm to my forehead.

"Kate, you're not going to kill yourself," said Paul, gently pushing me back to a normal sitting position and taking a sip from his large black coffee. His blue eyes looked at me steadily and a small smile formed at the corners of his mouth. He spoke with the slow confidence of someone who's never *not* gotten his way. "You're going to get into Yale and go there in the fall and do many things to me in my dorm room. Unspeakable things."

"Wrong," I said, trying not to laugh at his disappointed pout. I reached up to smooth down a piece of his hair. He hadn't gotten it cut in a while and a small light brown tendril was sticking out from under his Red Sox cap. "The application is due in two weeks and I still have no essay. Can't get in without an essay."

It wasn't for lack of trying. I'd been dreaming about Yale for three years, ever since Paul and I decided on going there together, so I'd obviously started thinking about the perfect personal statement forever ago. But I hadn't even come up with anything to write about, much less typed more than two sentences before deciding it sucked and erasing it in frustration.

"You just have writer's block," Paul said soothingly. His deep voice was calm as he squeezed my hand across the table. "Once you start I'm sure you'll write something great."

"Not as great as this," I sighed, waving my hand over the most perfect collection of five hundred words I'd ever read. "This is hilarious, but still sounds super smart. And it's such a memorable story. . . ." Paul and his friends had started a punk band when they were twelve, and he'd gotten a nasty infection while trying to give himself a tattoo. The essay's last line was about the scar he still sports, a tiny, paler patch of skin on his left bicep. It's barely noticeable, but certainly made for great essay fodder. The admissions officers would eat it up.

Meanwhile, I was serving them nothing.

I sighed and leaned back in my chair. I wanted so badly to pack my stuff into Paul's car and drive down I-95 to New Haven with him next year. But as the application deadline loomed, my already small chances were shrinking by the day. If I didn't get in, Paul and I would be apart, probably far apart. And when's the last time two college freshmen survived a long-distance relationship?

Yep, I had to get into Yale.

"I might not get in either," Paul pointed out. He picked up his essay and tucked it into his back pocket, as if putting it out of sight would put it out of my mind.

"HA!" I said way too loudly. The guy behind the counter and the kid in the corner wearing headphones both looked at me weirdly. "There is a zero percent chance of that. Your dad went to Yale. Both your grandfathers went to Yale. And they all donate. A lot."

"That doesn't guarantee anything," he reminded me.

I leaned forward and yanked on the end of one of his navy blue hoodie strings to even them out. "But you've got a 4.3 GPA. You're the captain of the basketball team. And you got a 2390 on the SATs. All that legacy stuff is just icing on the cake."

Paul smiled a little. "Well, if you really wanna play that game, you have a 4.1. You're the cocaptain of the volleyball team and you got a 2320," he countered. "Which, by the way, is an awesome score. I have no idea why you're doing it again."

"I want a 2370," I said flatly. I'd gotten that high on practice tests and figured I should give it another shot, even if it meant ending a brutal finals week with a hugely stressful standardized test. "Plus, there are at least five kids with 4.0s breathing down my 4.1 neck. One A-minus on finals and *boom*, I'm not third in the class. I'm eighth, behind six other known Yale applicants."

"You actually keep track of that stuff?" Paul asked, incredulous. I almost laughed, but then I would've had to explain the obsessive-compulsive nerdiness of the spreadsheet I constantly updated on my computer that told me these things.

"When our dream school has never admitted more than two kids from Colchester High in one year, yes, of course I keep track," I said matter-of-factly. "You're a shoo-in, whereas my shoes are aggressively out. I mean, how long did it even take you to write that?" I asked, pointing at his pocket. "An hour?"

Paul shrugged. "Something like that," he admitted.

"So? You have your on-campus interview coming up, and they'll love you. Just like I do." He grinned at me.

I took a deep breath and smiled weakly back at him. I doubted they'd love the shell of a human I was going to be after the upcoming two weeks of finals and SATs. I would have exactly one day to recover before my campus visit, and I was certain that it wouldn't be enough. One *month* might not be enough. "Thanks," I sighed.

"And if they don't," he said very seriously, grasping my hands and gazing into my eyes, "I will storm the admissions office armed with a tire iron. Or, more realistically, just get really angry and swear a lot." He grinned at me again, then drained his coffee cup and effortlessly arced it through the air into the trash can twenty feet away. "Ready?" he asked.

I nodded. Our little coffee break had already turned into a much longer study hiatus than my schedule allotted. That happens all the time when your boyfriend barely has to study to be valedictorian.

We put on our coats and walked out into the cold. It was nearly dark already, a typical December afternoon in suburban Boston, and a thin gray drizzle had started to come down. Paul clicked open the door of his black hybrid SUV and took out his phone so we could keep talking as we drove.

"Hey," I said into my cell as I unlocked the door to my

little blue Civic. As soon as I got in, I hit the speakerphone button, dropped the phone into my lap, and cranked the heat. Since I hate driving with gloves, I pulled my hands inside my coat sleeves and settled in to wait until the car warmed up.

"Okay, how's this," Paul continued. I saw his car pulling out of the lot toward his side of town. "You should just screw the essay and write them a letter. 'Dear Yale, my name is Katerina Larson, and you have to let me in because I'm extremely hot.'" I laughed while Paul kept talking. "'I've got gorgeous eyes and an even better body. Seriously, it's ridiculous. You know who else is hot? My boyfriend. He's six three and really jacked, even though he doesn't work out that much.'"

"You do work out that much," I reminded him, rubbing my palms together in front of the heater.

"They don't know that," he answered.

"Well, if you want to write it for me, be my guest," I said, easing my car out of the parking space. I drove slowly, since the late-afternoon drizzle was becoming evening freezing rain, making the empty, tree-lined streets trickier than usual to navigate.

"I might have to do that," Paul agreed. "Maybe then I can squeeze myself into your schedule." His tone was joking, but I could hear the slight annoyance underneath. Not that I blamed him—I'd definitely been MIA lately. Over the summer, we'd been together constantly, but after the school year started and my AP classes got more intense, we'd seen each other less and less. In fairness, Paul basically lived at basketball practice and his schedule wasn't exactly AP-light, but there was no doubt that I was the busier one.

"It's all for a good cause," I answered, trying to sound lighthearted. "Next year we'll have all the time in the world. Plus we've got winter break," I added. Neither of our families had vacation plans. In fact, I was pretty sure my mom had a business trip for part of it—I can never keep track. So I was looking forward to lazing around in front of the fireplace, renting movies, and drinking hot chocolate. I could just *relax*. For the first time in three years.

"So fourteen days," he said. "Fourteen days till I get my girlfriend back."

"Fourteen days," I agreed. "Start the countdown."

There was a long beat. "One."

"That's counting up," I pointed out.

"Damn, I was hoping I'd be able to trick you into thinking it was already over."

I giggled as I pulled into my driveway, tapping the clicker that opened the brick-colored garage door. "Nope, but I appreciate the effort. Maybe I'll write about it in my essay: 'My Boyfriend's Attempts to Convince Me of a Warp in the Space-Time Continuum.'"

"Well, it certainly makes you sound nerdy. I'd definitely let you in."

If only it were that easy.

TO-DO LIST

- Essay!
- SAT practice—at least 2 sections
- AP Euro flash cards
- Bio lab questions, go over project notebook
- French vocab, memorize dialogue, extra credit essay
- English—get copy of The Sound and the Fury, return Paul's
  Crime and Punishment
- Physics final—practice problem sets
- Prom committee crap (location rental, food/drink ideas,
  talk everyone out of hiring lame band, etc.)
- Volleyball flyer designs
- Yearbook superlatives, list possible categories?
- Christmas—tree? Presents (Mom, wallet; Paul, sweater???
  Mix CD for Kyla et al.)

POSSIBLE ESSAY TOPICS

"The Time in Ninth Grade That I Decided to Wear
  Mismatched Socks for a Month"

"Sophomore Year I Didn't Have to Wear Nearly as Supportive
  a Sports Bra as I Do Now"

"Note to Self: Back Up iTunes Next Time"

(Okay, maybe not)

CHAPTER TWO
MONDAY, DECEMBER 3

THE NEXT MORNING MY BEST FRIEND, KYLA, was camped out in front of my locker, two coffees in hand. "I drank most of mine already," she said, standing up and handing me a still-steaming cup. "I considered switching it with yours and then pretending to get all mad that Starbucks ripped us off, but I figured it would take too much acting energy too early in the morning. Although now that I'm caffeinated, I seem to have it. See?" She jumped up and down several times, making goofy faces at me.

"Morning," I answered dryly. We usually traded off coffee pickup days, but I'd been so busy lately she'd taken over. I took a huge swig out of my cup, hoping the heavily sugared liquid would give me the energy to deal with Kyla's usual rapid-fire delivery. She seemed even more hyper today than usual.

"So what's this I hear about you going into college app

panic?" Kyla asked, poking me in the ribs with her elbow while flipping her chin-length red hair out of her enviably porcelain-skinned face. "You know you can pull off one stupid little essay. I bet you're already on the last sentence."

I yanked my locker open. "First of all, it's not a 'little' essay. It's the most important thing I've ever written. And I haven't even started it yet."

"Of course you haven't—because you're confident you'll get it done." Kyla could make anything positive. She's one of those people who would be like, "Your boyfriend's cheating on you? It is *fabulous* that we found out! Now you can dump the bastard and we totally have more time to shop and watch *So You Think You Can Dance!*" It's a lovely quality, actually. Her other lovely quality is that we're the exact same size. So even though her clothing taste is on the hookery side, which I can say because she always claims I got beaten with the J. Crew stick, it's a great way to double our wardrobes.

"Why am I the only one worried about getting into college?" I asked. I slammed my bright blue locker door and my coffee cup splashed a few drops through the sippy hole in the cover. I slurped the spill off the plastic as we headed down the hallway toward AP English (me) and government (Kyla). Around us, the pre-bell rush of kids formed a dense blur of backpacks and groggy faces shuffling in random directions under chilly fluorescent lighting.

"Because," Kyla answered, stepping quickly to the side

as a gaggle of juniors squeezed past, "I get to go wherever I want since I am a fabulous, heavily recruited volleyball player. Whereas you are only a mediocre volleyball player, which is sad but true, and also something *you've* said before, so don't get mad at me. And the rest of our friends will be happy with state schools. And your boyfriend's family paid his way into Yale—"

"They're generous donors. It's not the same thing."

"It's exactly the same thing, but whatever. He's a genius so he deserves it anyway."

"Thank you."

"And finally because you're turning into a giant, high-strung nerd. Chill out! Smoke some pot. Just kidding—bad message, but chill out."

We paused at the door of my English class. "I'll try," I sighed, as I walked into the room.

"No, you won't," Kyla said over her shoulder, as she nimbly sidestepped people and wove her way through the crowded hallway.

At lunch I was hoping to hide in the library with an SAT practice section, but I was waylaid about ten steps from the cafeteria door by my guidance counselor, Ms. Renner. I love Ms. Renner. I respect Ms. Renner. But I also recognized the look on her face.

"Kate! Hi! I was wondering if you could do me a favor."

I winced inwardly but smiled. I couldn't say no, especially not after all the advice she's given me on classes and the best summer internships.

"Of course!" I said brightly.

"Fantastic. A couple students need help with their college application essays and I was wondering whether you could proofread a few of them, help them with grammar and things like that?"

Ugh. "Um, sure. I actually haven't started mine yet, but—"

"Oh, thank you! Don't worry, they're not . . ." She lowered her voice. "These kids aren't exactly Ivy-bound. It shouldn't take you too long. Thank you so much!" She pulled a sheaf of papers out of the pile of folders she was carrying and cheerfully handed them to me.

There went my lunchtime SAT practice.

Later, on my way into study hall, I ran into my volleyball coach, who is also the school newspaper advisor and was my English teacher freshman and sophomore years.

"Just the person I wanted to see," Coach Tate said breathlessly, brushing her frizzy gray-blond bangs out of her eyes. "Would you mind sitting in on a few freshman gym classes sometime this week? It'd be great to see if there's anybody I need to hassle about trying out for the team."

"Sure," I said, suppressing the urge to blurt, "For chrissakes, just pick all the tall chicks!" I couldn't turn down the woman who'd promised to write me the most glowing recommendation in her twenty-five-year teaching career.

"Thank you!" She smiled at me gratefully. "There's a class right now. I can excuse you from study hall to head over there."

So much for study hall.

Toward the end of the day, I tracked Paul down by his locker. "You could say no once in a while," he suggested after I recounted Ms. Renner and Coach Tate's favors. "But you won't—that's just how you roll," he finished, smiling and shaking his head a little as I threw my arms up helplessly. "And I love that about you."

"Do you love that I never sleep?" I muttered under my breath.

"What?"

"Nothing," I sighed. "Also, I just heard that I'm running the yearbook meeting before school on Friday, because Sierra's out with chicken pox," I added.

"Sierra Lenz has chicken pox *now*? She's eighteen!"

"That's what *I* said."

"Well, you can handle it, but please don't forget all this." Paul playfully gestured at himself from head to toe, and I felt a pang of guilt knowing that I was putting him further down my task list than he should be. I needed a personal assistant. Or possibly two. Or one of those Harry Potter time-turner gizmos so I could do multiple things at once.

By the time last period rolled around I was in a colossally bad mood. I rushed into AP physics slightly late, thanks to my locker deciding to get stuck open until I violently kicked the door, injuring both it and my big toe. Luckily nobody noticed, because they were too busy applauding our teacher.

"What?" I whispered to Anne Conroy, as I slid into the other seat at her lab table. "Did something happen?"

"Mr. Piper said there wasn't gonna be a final," she whispered back, her round face, a contrast to her reed-thin body, still half-turned toward the front of the room. She reached up to re-tighten her already-taut, straw-colored ponytail.

"Shut. Up," I said. No physics final? Oh my God, all the time I'd mentally budgeted to study was suddenly free! This was just the break I needed! My eyes widened and I stared at Anne, openmouthed, then turned to look at Mr. Piper. His gray hair was even more mussed than usual and he was rubbing his hands together, looking positively gleeful.

"As I was saying," he said, "this semester, instead of a final exam . . ."

The entire class suddenly groaned as we all realized that there was a catch—of course.

"There will be a final *project*," Mr. Piper continued.

Oh no. Oh *no.*

Silence. Somebody in the back row muttered a very small "boo," decided that it had been too small, and then muttered, "Boo!" again, louder.

"Your partners will be assigned and you'll draw projects out of a hat," he went on.

God, this sucked. This sucked *big-time.*

Somebody raised their hand. "Why can't we pick our partners?"

"I'm very aware that you and your girlfriend are both in this class, Mr. Rosenrock, but I'm sorry. I purposely assigned it randomly. So without further ado . . ." Mr. Piper started reading names off a list. Bleh. I didn't particularly care that we couldn't pick partners, I just hoped mine was smart. I needed that A. Without it, my GPA—and therefore Yale—was shot.

"Kate Larson and Jake Cheng."

Well, so much for Yale.

I slowly gathered my stuff, but Jake was on his way over to my lab table already. He threw down a beat-up notebook with multicolored pencil and ink doodles all over the cover, then yawned noisily and chucked a physics textbook, also covered in doodles, on top of it.

"Hey Jake," I said.

"Wow," he said sarcastically. "Kate Larson remembers my name."

Oh, so this was how it was gonna be. I checked to see whether his sarcastic tone had been followed by a dazzlingly friendly smile. Nope.

"Of course I remember you," I said patiently. We'd gone to the same school since kindergarten. "You don't consider yourself memorable?"

"To the right audience, of course," Jake said, crossing his arms. He was a few inches taller than me—he must've grown a bunch since the last time I'd paid any attention. "To the queen of the school . . ." He plunked his thin, wiry frame down in his chair, yanked at the collar of his faded Patriots Super Bowl T-shirt for a second, then kicked his feet onto the table and clasped his hands behind his head.

"What's that supposed to mean?" I asked, glaring at him.

"It means—"

"Kate, will you do the honors?" Mr. Piper held out a beaker filled with little slips of paper. I reached in and pulled one out.

"Robotic catapult," I read.

"Excellent!" Mr. Piper said. "Trajectories and precision of movement will be fun for you two." He walked off to the next table as Jake rolled his eyes. I rolled mine too as I sat back down. *Fun* wasn't exactly the word that came to mind.

"It means," Jake said, finishing his thought from before Piper's interruption, "that you used to be normal and chill,

and now you're all hard-core and 'eeeehhhh!'" He spasti-
cally waved his hands back and forth as he made that high-
pitched last sound, clearly demonstrating that he thought I
was some sort of neurotic academic supernerd. "Like I can
already tell you're gonna be all gung-ho about getting an A
on this thing."

"Of course I want an A," I said evenly. "Actually, I need it."

"Exactly. Whereas I'm cool with a C." Jake raised an
eyebrow at me as if daring me to say something.

"Well that's great," I said, trying to keep the irritation
out of my voice. Maybe my essay could be a detailed account
of plotting and carrying out the cold-blooded murder of
my lab partner. Why was Jake being so annoying?

"So," he asked conversationally, "how pissed is your
boyfriend gonna be that we're lab partners?"

Oh, right. That was why.

"He's not gonna be pissed," I said with forced patience.

"Oh really? The guy who told you to quit hanging out
with me three years ago?" Jake narrowed his dark, almost-
black eyes.

"Oh my God, that is *so* not what happened," I said
fiercely. Jake and I had been really good friends as kids. But
in high school, I was put into all accelerated classes while
he'd taken an artsier route, so we'd kind of naturally started
hanging out less. Then Paul and I had met in honors bio
and he'd gently pointed out that playing video games in

Jake's basement all day wasn't really going to get me into an Ivy League school. It wasn't like Jake and I had suddenly stopped talking—it had been more of a gradual fade.

"We drifted apart, Jake." I shrugged. "It happens when people get to high school. I mean, we're not friends with Erica Kirk anymore either."

"Of course we're not—she's a total bitch."

"I know," I agreed, smiling. But Jake's angular face remained stony. He stared into space, absently running his hand over his close-cropped black hair for a moment. He then picked up a silver Sharpie and started drawing a little cartoon vampire on the dull black surface of the lab table.

"I saw that, Mr. Cheng," said Mr. Piper, walking toward us. "Detention."

Jake swore under his breath and stopped drawing as Piper threw our project folders onto the table with a thunk. I picked mine up and flipped through it quickly, wincing. Charts. Graphs. Statistics. Instructions. The assignment described building a contraption that would roll over to a Ping-Pong ball, pick it up, and throw it at three different targets. I didn't have the first idea on how to begin. Neither did Jake, as he hadn't even bothered to open his folder. He was busy drawing a mutated, frothing-at-the-mouth gerbil on the front cover.

I looked around the classroom. At every other table, people already had rulers and calculators out and were jotting down notes with their partners.

The hell with it. "Look," I said to Jake. "It's not your fault we haven't talked in three years, but it's not totally mine either. So quit being so annoying."

He stopped drawing. "Less than three years, technically," he answered. "I said hi to you in the hallway once and you just walked on by."

"Did not," I retorted. "Or if I did, it's because I didn't hear you."

"Of course. You were probably too busy hanging out with the cheerleading squad."

"Volleyball team," I corrected him.

"Same difference," he answered.

"It's actually extremely easy to tell those two groups of people apart," I snapped.

"Oh, right," he said, "volleyball's got that seven-foot lesbian on it."

"No, that would be the cheerleaders." Well, she was technically six one and not a lesbian, but she did have extremely short hair. She would definitely be on the bottom of the pyramid if our cheerleading squad ever did pyramids. Mostly they just do booty dances.

"Sorry, guess I'm not as clued in to the inner workings of this school as you are," Jake said. "Some of us didn't sell out as soon as we got to high school and started dating Mr."—he made his voice into a dopey-sounding singsong—"HarvardPrincetonYaaaaale."

"I don't give a damn what you think of me, my boyfriend, or this school: I just wanna make sure I'm not working on this by myself," I said, stabbing my finger toward one of the robot diagrams.

"You won't be," Jake shrugged. "You just might not be getting an A." The bell rang and he got up and left, not even bothering to take his project folder with him.

I glared at the empty space where Jake used to be and a new personal statement idea formed in my mind. Yep. "The Time I Killed My Physics Lab Partner and Got Away With It, at Least Until I Wrote This Essay" definitely had potential.

CHAPTER THREE

"GO TO BED, WOMAN." MY MOM POKED HER head in my bedroom door. "It's nearly midnight."

I sighed and leaned back in my desk chair. I was clad in flannel pajama pants and a hoodie, my hair pulled back into a messy "study mode" bun. I'd slogged through all my homework, plus an extra credit French essay to make up for the A-minus I'd gotten on a quiz last week, and two practice SAT math sections. I'd also taken a halfhearted shot at my personal statement, but as usual hadn't gotten any further than typing a few new titles. Not that "Highlights or Lowlights? The Brunette's Dilemma" was going to be a winner.

"Why should I go to bed if you're not?" I asked, swallowing a yawn. I had been wired on three cans of Diet Coke and some leftover chocolate toffee cheesecake, but by this point "wired" had turned into "barely conscious."

"I am as soon as I finish reviewing these," my mom answered, holding up a thick black binder. She was wearing her reading glasses, and her dark, wavy hair was held out of her face with one of my plastic claw-shaped hair clips. "Which will take less than half an hour, because I am the smartest lawyer ever. So go to bed."

"I will," I said. "Right after I take another crack at this Yale essay."

My mom came farther into the room to peer at my computer monitor. "Write about your wonderful mom," she said.

"Paul already suggested 'write about your awesome boyfriend,'" I answered, smiling.

"Damn, that kid is smart."

"Yeah, I may just get him to do the whole thing for me. Wanna help?" I asked. My mom got her BA and PhD from Columbia, and then went to Harvard Law. Which made her great to look up to and impossible to live up to. Not that she would ever point that out.

"Would if I could, kiddo," my mom said dryly. "Well, good luck." She kissed me on the forehead and then left, closing the door behind her.

Beep. An IM popped up on my screen from Paul that said, **Hey sexy. Oh wait, that's me.**

I laughed, then grabbed my cell off the dresser and called him.

"Aha," Paul said as soon as he picked up. "You want nothing more than to hear my soulful voice."

"No." I sighed. "I want nothing more than to be asleep right now, but that's not an option." I flopped onto the bed, tucking my feet under one corner of my green and white striped comforter. Nothing in my room matches. The carpet is pale blue, the wallpaper yellow flowers, the furniture a mix of Ikea and oak. But it's cozy and spacious at the same time, and I love it.

"Aw, poor baby," Paul said. "So go to bed. You're probably done with your essay by now, right?"

"Nope. Blank page. No words. Very sad." I glanced at the clock and sighed. "Plus I have to read through this entire physics assignment since I know Jake's not going to."

"No kidding. I hate that you have to work with that kid."

"Oooh, jealous?" I teased.

"Of a guy I could break in half?" Paul laughed. "No, but be careful or he's gonna drag your grade down."

"It'll be fine," I said, trying to convince myself. Actually, it probably wasn't going to be fine at all, but I'd complained to Paul enough lately.

"Too bad you couldn't choose partners. Then you could've just worked with Anne."

"Yeah . . ." I agreed, even though I didn't. Anne's really smart—she's got a 4.07 and is also applying to Yale—but she's more Paul's friend than mine. Actually, she and Paul dated freshman year. It was only for a few weeks, and it was long before he and I got together, but the fact that they've stayed such good friends is . . . well . . . annoying. Especially since it's obvious—to me, at any rate—that she still has a thing for him.

"Well, I should get back to work," I said, trying to sound chipper.

"Anything I can do to help?"

"Yes," I answered, getting up and stretching. "Boost my mood and self-esteem by whispering sweet nothings in my ear."

Paul laughed. "Oh, I'll whisper stuff. I'll whisper sweet *somethings*."

A few minutes later we hung up and I looked at the clock. Now it was well past midnight. So if I stayed up until two, then woke up at six, I'd get four hours of sleep. Which, sadly, was about average lately. I looked at my computer monitor. A blank white Word document stared back at me. Ugh. I minimized the window, quickly checked cuteoverload-dot-com (awww, an extremely fat kitten!), and then stared at my computer desktop. Icons of barely started essays were scattered haphazardly across the screen. I closed my eyes and the icons swirled around, taunting me.

"Go away," I muttered. I started deleting the icons—no

point starting an essay with a messy desktop, right? Ah, productive procrastination. I erased "volleyball essay" and "library essay" and "friendship essay" and "killing Jake essay." I had started that one right after I got home from school, although it fizzled at the three-sentence mark, at which point I'd already used the word *douchebag* four times.

Click-drag. Click-drag. Click-drag. My desktop got cleaner by the second as I started deleting old shortcuts and random downloads. It felt cathartic, and the methodical task helped wake me up. Maybe there was something in here to write about, something about a blank slate, or starting from scratch, or . . . My mind whirled as I deleted.

I sat back to admire my work. Yay! Or boo, since now I had to start writing. Dammit. I pointed the cursor at my blank word document again, then noticed one last icon, a colorful little script "SL" with a smiley face on it, in the corner of the screen.

"Don't know what it is, don't need it," I said, and moved it to the trash.

It bounced out of the trash and went back to its former spot.

I put it back in the trash.

It bounced right back out.

"Oh, come on," I muttered. I highlighted it and hit "delete." Nothing happened. I tried again. Nothing. I trashed it again, and suddenly a window popped open that said, "Welcome to SimuLife!"

Sigh.

I tried to close the window, but a weird, tinny music cue sounded and the program stayed open. The noise was jarring in the late-night silence of my room, and I winced and turned the computer speakers down.

What the hell was SimuLife still doing on my computer, anyway? I vaguely remembered playing the game back in the day, but I hadn't touched it in years. I made a mental note to tell my mom that this was yet another reason I needed a new computer, then wiggled the mouse. The whole screen was frozen. I checked the clock; Paul was definitely asleep by now, and I didn't want to wake him just for computer help. I looked over at my crappy old laptop lying on the floor by the closet. It would have to do.

I turned back to my computer and hit control-alt-delete in a last-ditch attempt. Once, then twice.

Nothing. The SimuLife window was still stuck open.

Screw the laptop, I was going to bed. The universe clearly didn't want me to work on my essay. For once the universe and I were in agreement.

TO-DO LIST

- Essay!
- SAT practice—~~at least 2 sections~~ 2 MORE SECTIONS
- AP Euro flash cards
- Bio ~~lab questions~~, go over project notebook
- ~~French vocab, memorize dialogue, extra credit essay~~
- ~~English—get copy of THE SOUND AND THE FURY, return Paul's CRIME AND PUNISHMENT~~
- Physics ~~final—practice problem sets~~ STUPID $%#!$@! ROBOT
- Prom committee crap (~~location rental~~, food/drink ideas, talk everyone out of hiring lame band, etc.)
- Volleyball flyer designs and e-mail Coach Tate re: freshmen
- Yearbook superlatives, list possible categories—MEETING FRIDAY MORNING
- Christmas—tree? presents (Mom, wallet; Paul, sweater??? Mix CD for Kyla et al.)
- Essay, and I really mean it this time!
- Other people's essays for Renner (oh, the irony)

REMINDERS!

* Fix computer; if not fixable, call school IT guy
* Purple vitamin water for Paul bball practice
* Get blank CDs
* Run w/Kyla, return her blue tank (wash it first) (or maybe don't bother since she didn't with my cords)

*** WRITE. STUPID. ESSAY. DAMMIT. ***

CHAPTER FOUR
TUESDAY, DECEMBER 4

FWAMP. FWAMP. FWAMP. I REACHED TO SLAM the snooze button on my alarm clock and realized that both my arms were completely tangled in the blankets. I wiggled around to free myself and finally turned off the alarm, then snuggled back under the covers. I was just drifting back to blissful early-morning half-sleep when I heard a voice.

"Don't you think you should get up already?"

"What? No," I said, not bothering to open my eyes. "There's a snooze button for a reason." I was halfway asleep again when I realized that the voice did not belong to my mother.

There was someone in my room.

I'm not gonna lie, I shrieked bloody murder. Then I scooched backwards across my bed as fast as I could and scrunched up against the wall, my body in an upright fetal position, my heels on one of my pillows. I held another pillow in front of me, like that would save me, and struggled to keep myself from breathing either way too hard or not at all.

But the stranger in my room was a teenage girl. About five six, wavy dark brown hair falling just past her shoulders, brown eyes, a decent complexion. Couple freckles on the cheekbones. She was smiling, and she wasn't holding a gun or a knife. All in all, if there was going to be a random stranger in your room, this was not a bad person for her to look like.

Except that she looked exactly like me.

"What the hell?" I screeched. "Mom!"

"She left for work," the girl said sunnily. "Hi!"

"Hi?" I replied, surveying my room frantically. Everything looked the same as usual: piles of books on the floor, clothes draped on every surface, random pens and pencils scattered on my desk and dresser, the edge of my computer monitor covered in Post-it notes. The door to my walk-in closet was open, which was weird because I always closed it at night, and the overhead light was on even though I hadn't left my bed yet, but otherwise everything looked normal.

Except for the girl. Who looked like me.

"I'm hallucinating," I said out loud. "This is why one should always say no to drugs."

But I *had* said no to drugs!

"Who the hell are you?" I demanded. I was still backed up against the wall, and the girl happily settled herself at the foot of my bed, sitting cross-legged and hugging one of my pillows. "Don't touch my stuff," I added. She put the pillow down.

"What, seriously? You don't know?" the girl asked. "I'm Rina!"

I stared at her blankly.

"Rina," she repeated. Another blank stare from me. "Nice to meet you," the girl continued. "Or me, I guess." She giggled.

"You're not me," I said. Except that she kind of was. Actually, she totally was, except for the fact that instead of flannel jammie pants and a T-shirt, she had on a fuzzy pink tracksuit and a ton of lip gloss. And body glitter. Her cheekbones and the backs of her hands were completely covered in body glitter. Ew, tacky.

When in doubt and fearing for your own sanity, be rude. "What kind of a freak name is Rina?" I demanded.

"Um, the freak name you gave me 'cause you thought it was a cooler nickname for Katerina than Kate," she said. "I couldn't believe you signed on last night! Finally! It's been forever!" She pointed happily at my computer. I looked too. It was still frozen, the "Welcome to SimuLife!" window stuck open.

Oh no. Wait. The wheels turned in my head. . . .

SimuLife—what kind of a game was SimuLife? And what did it have to do with this girl in my—oh. *Uh-oh.*

She was the version of me from the game. In theory, it made no sense, but the reality sort of made sense. Leave it to my hallucination to sort of make sense. "So . . . you're my SimuLife self?" I asked shakily, blinking a few times in a mixture of confusion and horror.

"Yeah!" Rina nodded happily. "I knew we were smart! Thanks for busting me out. The last time we saw each other was what, eighth grade?"

"I didn't bust you out," I snapped, relaxing enough to sink down onto one of my pillows instead of staying slammed up against the wall. "I clearly have dormant schizophrenia and it's just manifesting itself at the most stressful time of my life."

"No, we're sane," Rina said cheerfully, the light reflecting off her glittery cheeks. She crawled toward me, stuck out a finger, and poked me in the stomach.

"Ow! What the hell?!" I yelled, shrinking away.

"You're not hallucinating." She looked around. "So now what?"

"What do you mean, now what? I have no idea." I took a deep breath, willing myself to calm down, even as I freaked out again at the sight of me sitting across from myself. She was even twisting the ends of her hair with one hand like I do, curling the waves into loose ringlets. "There has to be an explanation for this," I said. "A perfectly reasonable, rational, scientific explanation."

"Why?" Rina asked.

"Because this isn't the way the world works!" I exclaimed. "If it is, then there might as well be superheroes. And zombies. And goblins and talking plants and magic lamps that grant wishes—"

"Maybe there are," Rina said. "Oh my God, how cool would that be? I would wish for a new car, and a bunch of new clothes, and—"

"Me too," I said without thinking. Rina looked at me, delighted that I'd agreed with her, and I slapped myself on the forehead. What was I doing? We stared at each other for a moment; then my alarm clock went off again. Thanks, snooze button. The repetitive blare gave me a sudden moment of clarity.

I jumped off my bed, walked over to my computer, and yanked out the power cord. Ta-da! The screen went black. Goodbye, SimuLife! Goodbye, weird girl in my room!

I turned around. Rina was still there.

Dammit.

"Okay, I can't deal with this right now," I said. "I'm about to be late for school. I haven't showered, none of my stuff is together—" I started walking around the room, picking books and papers off the floor and cramming them into my book bag. I had to get out of here. Maybe outside the house, everything would be normal.

"Can I come to school?" asked Rina, getting up from the bed as I went into the closet to figure out what to wear.

"What?" I asked, kicking off my jammie pants and pulling on some jeans. "Of course not! Are you completely insane?" I started putting on a long-sleeved T-shirt and noticed through the window the sprinkling of snow on the lawn, then pulled on one of Paul's Red Sox hoodies instead.

Rina made a sad face at me. God, it was so, so weird looking at her; not like looking in the mirror, but more like looking at a photo come to life. I mean, was my hair doing the same thing as hers? One piece on the left side was kind of sticking out. I reached toward my head. "Your hair looks good," Rina said. "Oh, but is there something wrong with mine?" She ran her hand through her hair in the exact same motion I'd just made. Great, this was getting even weirder.

I sighed and looked at the clock. "Look," I said, "If you're still around later—"

"Of course I'll be around!"

I sighed again. "Okay, just—just stay in here. I'll be back at, like, three, and we can figure out what to do then."

"I have to stay in our room? I can't even go down-stairs?" she asked.

"First of all it's my room, not ours, and no, you can't.

Watch YouTube or iTunes or something. You'll have to plug the computer back in. Just promise you'll stay here."

Rina shrugged. "Okay."

"Thanks." I took a deep breath, closed my eyes, made a wish, and opened them again. Rina waved at me.

So much for that. I picked up my book bag and started for the door.

"Hey Kate?" Rina asked.

"What?"

"The last time you played SimuLife was in eighth grade," she said.

"So?" I asked.

"So isn't it great that we grew boobs since then?"

I almost laughed before catching myself. "Yeah, I guess," I said, smiling a little at the hilariously contented look on Rina's face. "Okay. I'm leaving now. Don't go anywhere."

"Okay. Bye Kate!" Rina waved enthusiastically.

"Bye."

I went downstairs and picked up my car keys from the front hall table, wondering whether it was a good idea for a clinically insane person to drive herself to school. Maybe I should head to the emergency room instead.

Nope. Too much work to do.

"Have a great day at school!" called Rina's voice from upstairs. *My* voice. Granted, it sounded like my voice when it's on voice mail, so it wasn't exactly what I heard in my head. But it was still way too familiar to be coming from anywhere except my own mouth.

"Kate?" Rina's voice repeated. "Have a great day at school!"

Something told me she would just say it again until I responded. "Thanks!" I finally called back.

"Can't wait to see you later!"

I couldn't say the same.

Dear Diary,

The real world is AWESOME! Kate's room is SO COOL!!
AAAAAAAAAAAAAAAAAHHHHHHHHHHHH!!!!!!!!!!!
YAY! YAY YAY YAY YAY YAY!
This. Is. The happiest day of my life. Except for the time I
accidentally ate glitter gloss and thought I might die but then didn't.

Love, Rina

CHAPTER FIVE

"WHOA, WHAT'S WRONG?" PAUL ASKED ME, shortly after I got to school.

I wasn't sure how I'd gotten from the parking lot to my locker, or how I'd remembered the combination once I was there. And I definitely wasn't sure how I'd ended up on the ground.

"Huh? What?" I looked up at him. He was wearing a Red Sox hoodie, which meant we matched. Great, now I had a twin at home *and* at school. Of course, he looked way better in his than I did in mine, although he probably would've disagreed. He's good that way.

"You're sitting in the middle of the hallway," Paul said.

I looked around and saw a mass of knees and calves and feet. Paul was exaggerating—I was on the floor, yes, but I was leaning back against my locker. I pulled my feet in just as a crowd of laughing sophomore guys stomped by.

Paul extended a hand. I let him yank me to a standing position, which he did with almost zero effort. "Sorry," I said blurrily. "I'm just a little out of it." That was an understatement.

"Are you okay? Did you not go to sleep last night?" His eyes looked concerned, and he took one of my hands in his and waggled my arm around energetically.

"No, I did," I said. "But I've just—I've got a lot on my mind." Specifically, the fact that I was mentally ill.

This was a bummer.

Although, if I played my cards right, an essay about dealing with mental illness might make for a pretty sweet college application. . . .

See, thinking of using my insanity to get into college just proved that I was crazy.

"Kate," Paul said, gently turning my face toward him. I gazed into his blue eyes for a second, forcing myself not to think about staring into my own brown eyes, but on someone else's face, earlier this morning.

"Hi, yes, I'm here. Let's go to class," I said, shaking my head.

"We're already there," Paul said. Apparently, he'd walked us to AP English. He steered me through the door and into my seat, then sat down in the last row. He used to sit right behind me, but Ms. Appenfore made him switch because his height blocked the kids behind him. She likes to have a clear view of everyone, ever since the Great Senior Class Cell Phone–Throwing Incident. (Short version: somebody threw a cell phone.)

I looked around, wondering what the next sign that I was losing my proverbial marbles would be. Would Ms. Appenfore's head suddenly morph into a giant potato? Would the entire room turn into a black-and-white pencil drawing? Maybe everyone would start speaking Mandarin, or forty clowns would come busting out of the ceiling tiles (scary), or the voice of Daffy Duck would instruct me to pick up a black Magic Marker and draw a mustache on every kid in the room.

But Ms. Appenfore just droned on about *Crime and Punishment*. People raised their hands and answered her questions. Pages were turned, pens clicked. Everything was so . . . normal.

Maybe Rina had just been a bad dream. Oh my God, yes, that was it! Duh! I grinned at the thought, earning a "What's so funny, Kate?" from Ms. Appenfore. She was justified, as she had just referenced *Heart of Darkness*, which isn't exactly a laugh riot. I mouthed, "Nothing, sorry," and then looked down at my desk, smiling to myself. I wasn't nuts. I just had a vivid nocturnal imagination. REM sleep, you sly little dog, you.

My hand was resting on my desk. I spotted a few specks of body glitter on it.

Dammit, Rina.

I flicked the glitter off. Whatever, that might've come from anywhere. Maybe I'd walked by an art class at some point. Maybe I'd accidentally brushed against a slutty freshman. It could still all have been a dream. Right?

"Kate."

I looked up, and there was Paul, looking at me weirdly again. I realized that the bell had rung. "You're still totally out of it. Are you sure you're okay?" he asked, legitimate concern in his voice.

"Yeah, I'm fine," I said, hastily wiping away a few more specks of glitter.

"Do you want to go home? Are you sick?" Paul tucked my books under his arm to carry them for me, his face a mixture of worry and confusion. "I've never seen you like this. . . ."

That was true. I generally did a better job of acting normal in front of Paul—and everyone else—when I was stressed. Of course, I'd never had my computer avatar come to life before, which demanded way more acting talent than I had.

"I'm just sleepy," I said, throwing my pen into my bag. "I'll get a Diet Coke from the vending machine and I'll be fine. Don't worry."

"I'm going to anyway."

That was nice of him.

* * *

"Dude, what happened to you?" Kyla asked when I sat down next to her in AP European history. "Is something wrong? You totally look like something's wrong but you're trying to cover it up."

"Nothing's wrong," I lied wearily.

"Are you sure? You look . . . shell-shocked." Kyla's eyes narrowed as she studied me intently.

"I'm fine," I said. It occurred to me that Rina had been alone for a few hours now and for all I knew, she'd wrecked the house. For all I knew, she had *taken* the house, or at least all the stuff in it. Oh my God, what if Rina was a shape-shifter? Like, her normal body was some sort of monster, but she'd managed to disguise herself to gain trust while also making me think I was going crazy? What if right this second she was packing all my mom's jewelry and emergency cash, and our new big-screen TV, and everything else in the house, into a huge truck?

"I am zero percent convinced that nothing's wrong," said Kyla. "You look terrible."

I totally believed her there. I'm pretty sure the expression on my face at the thought of Rina being a shape-shifting house burglar could be described as "stricken."

"Well, then looking terrible is what's wrong, and thanks a lot for pointing it out," I replied, trying to sound confident but mostly just sounding loud. A few kids looked at me funny.

"Sorry. I'm kidding, you look great," she said. "Forget I said anything; I'm the worst friend ever for saying anything."

"It's okay, don't worry about it," I said, leaning my chin onto my hands. "I'm just a little stressed."

"Kate, I'm saying this as your best friend. If you're stressed enough to look like *that*, maybe you shouldn't retake the SATs. Because I'm afraid you might wind up having to check into a rehab facility for quote-unquote 'exhaustion,' and that'll just be the worst thing since—"

I was almost glad when Mr. Pike decided to give us a pop quiz on the life of Louis XIV.

By lunchtime I was robotically repeating, "I have a migraine," as my lame excuse for being totally out of it. "I took some Advil—I'll be fine," I told Kyla as I got up from our table after eating only a third of my turkey sandwich. "I'm gonna do some more SAT cramming." She nodded and waved. She's used to me holing up in the library at lunch lately, so I think she took it as a sign of normalcy. I handed the rest of my sandwich, plus my peanut butter Luna bar and banana, to our friend Carmen, whose appetite is scarily bottomless.

"We're hanging this weekend, right?" Carmen asked, as she started peeling the banana.

"Sure," I called back over my shoulder distractedly, as I was already halfway to where Paul was sitting with the basketball team. He stood up to meet me.

"Feeling better?" Paul asked, reaching over to brush my hair out of my face.

"Better enough to study," I said, indicating the SAT book in my bag. "I'm going to the library."

"That's my girl," Paul said, smiling. "I'll see you at practice later. You're still coming, right?" he asked, his smile fading at the "huh?" look on my face.

Right. Basketball practice. I'd promised to swing by, but I'd forgotten until he mentioned it.

"Of course," I answered. "I'll be there." I briefly pondered citing how busy I was in order to get out of it, but I needed to make up for acting so cracked out this morning.

"I mean, I know you've got all your other stuff, but you always—"

"Absolutely," I said quickly. I gave him a hug and made a mental note to get him a Vitamin Water after school. I made another mental note to tell Kyla I couldn't go running with her—even without basketball practice, I wouldn't have the time. Then I headed for the library.

I walked straight past the big wooden tables and squishy armchairs in the front section, past all the bookshelves and study rooms, and holed up in one of the back computer carrels. There, I googled the hell out of schizophrenia, hallucinations, delusions, multiple personality disorder, and anything else that might explain me having a vision of a clone that I could talk to and touch. The research was very educational, and also extremely depressing. I pictured a lifetime of institutionalization, being on eight medications at once, and my mom having the option to come visit me once a month but then only doing it once a year because she found the whole thing too much of a downer.

The future looked bleak. And I still had to get through the rest of the day without having a nervous breakdown.

"You look like crap," Jake said flatly as I sat down in physics.

"Well, you, um, smell like crap," I countered. He gave me a "wow, that's lame" eyebrow raise. "I barely slept and I have a headache," I snapped.

"Aww, let me guess. Your eighth retake of the SATs getting you down?" Jake made a mock sympathetic face. Around us, everyone else was huddled with their partners, calculators and diagrams in hand. My heart sank. If this thing was graded on a curve, we'd definitely be getting a C. Or worse. The look that I caught Anne giving me from across the room—a mixture of amusement and satisfaction—didn't help.

"First retake," I said defensively, "so shut up." I scooched my chair as far away from him as our lab table allowed. "And no," I added, glaring, "I actually haven't even had time to study for the SATs lately, since some of us have more to do than play with crayons all day." Jake was actually holding a red pencil at the moment, not a crayon, but whatever.

"You will regret that comment mightily when my brilliant artistic endeavors make me rich and famous," he said calmly. "Or at least rich." He twirled the pencil through his fingers and then quickly sketched a tongue-sticking-out face on my notebook.

"Nobody gets rich off art," I answered, snatching the notebook away from him. "Not until they're dead."

"Wrong. My exhibit A is the entire company of Pixar, and my exhibit B is that guy who makes sculptures out of Legos, and I could name a bunch of other people who've turned artistic ability into mountains of cash. But you're entitled to your factually incorrect opinion." Jake yanked up the sleeve of the green and blue flannel he was wearing over a Transformers T-shirt and used a ballpoint pen to draw a sneaker-clad praying mantis on his arm. He then drew a thought bubble over the mantis and wrote "KATE SUCKS!" in it.

I sighed deeply and closed my eyes. "Jake," I said. "Can't you just be nice to me? It would probably take less energy."

He cracked a hint of a smile. "I don't know, I'm pretty energy-efficient."

"Please," I said. "I'm having a rough day and you know it."

"Everyone who's seen your busted-ass face knows it."

"Exactly. So be a pal, okay?" Mr. Piper had just dumped a cardboard box filled with random pieces of metal and what looked like the insides of a computer onto our lab table, and the prospect of actually building something out of it was freaking me out almost as much as the thought of going home to find Rina still there.

Jake threw down his pen and waited a long beat. "I'll consider it."

"That's the best I'm gonna get from you today, huh?" I said wearily.

"Today, yeah," he answered, grinning at me. He picked a square of metal out of the cardboard box. "Do you care if I decorate the outside of our robot when we're done?"

"Oooh. Did you just admit you're going to help me build it?"

He paused slightly. "Yes."

"Oh my God, then yeah, go ahead, decorate it however the hell you want."

Jake got out a black Sharpie and promptly drew boobs on the piece of metal he was holding.

Fantastic.

CHAPTER SIX

I DRUMMED MY FINGERS NERVOUSLY ON THE steering wheel as I waited for a red light to change on my way home from school. I couldn't decide if I wanted to get home quickly, see that Rina wasn't there, and be relieved that it was all a bad dream, or get home slowly in case she was there. Why couldn't the weird thing in my life be a fairy godmother, or the sudden acquisition of magical powers? Either of those would be way more convenient.

The light turned green just as my phone beeped with a text message. "Dammit," I muttered, easing the car past a small patch of ice on the street. I waited until I got to the next red light, then dug in my bag for the phone. The text was from Paul and read, **Where r u?**

Oops. Clearly not at basketball practice.

The light turned green and I stepped on the gas, then hit the speakerphone button and called Paul back.

"Hey, this is Paul. Leave a message, thanks." *Beep*.

"Hey!" I said, my voice way too high and squeaky. I cleared my throat. "Oh my God, I'm so, so sorry! I totally forgot, and I'm not giving you an excuse, because I don't have one. I just forgot, and I'm sorry. I suck." I couldn't believe that basketball practice was something I had on both my physical and mental to-do lists, and I'd still screwed it up. "I'm the worst girlfriend in the world," I continued, "and I promise I will make it up to you somehow. Promise promise promise pr—aah!" A car suddenly pulled in front of me from the other lane and I had to slam on the brakes. "Asshole!" I yelled toward the windshield, before aiming my voice back toward the phone, which had fallen somewhere near my feet. "Hi again," I said loudly, hoping my voice carried down to the floor mat. "Sorry, this car just—anyway. Um. Sorry. Call me later."

My phone beeped again as I pulled into my driveway. It was another text from Paul: Its okay dont worry about it. love u.

Yay, he wasn't mad! Or at least not enough to pick a text fight. I sighed with relief and sent love u! as a reply.

Then I looked at my front door.

"Please let no one be in there," I said out loud. *Unless it's Mom*, I mentally added, but I knew it wouldn't be—she generally works until at least nine-thirty. Besides, her car was gone.

I unlocked the door and surveyed the front hall. Then I looked toward the kitchen and living room. Everything was empty and silent. I shrugged off my coat, hung it up, went up to my room, walked in the door, and—

"Hi!" said Rina.

Crap.

"Hi," I said wearily. I let my bag drop to the floor and winced when I realized that my laptop was in it. Luckily, it had fallen onto a pile of clothes. In fact, the entire floor was a pile of clothes. Every single item in my wardrobe had been liberated from hangers and drawers and strewn haphazardly around the room.

"Rina," I said, trying not to scream, "What did you do?"

"I tried on clothes!" she said cheerfully. "Do you like my outfit?"

She was wearing a red and black bikini top over a white racer-back tank, dusty blue cargo pants rolled up to the knee, green-and-gray argyle socks, and the strappy silver heels I'd worn to junior prom. Her hair was in pigtails and she was using a pair of my sunglasses as a headband.

"Your clothes are awesome," Rina said.

"Um . . . thanks," I said. "You look . . ." I didn't bother finishing the sentence.

Rina plopped down on my bed and waved the book she'd apparently been reading. There was an orange bookmark stuck about half an inch into it. "This is really good," she said.

"That's a thesaurus," I said.

"I know, it's really good!"

"Oh my God, how *dumb* are you?" I'd figured out that being rude to Rina didn't dampen her mood.

"I'm not," Rina answered cheerily. "I'm really smart, like you. I learned a lot of stuff today. Plus, there weren't any books in my house, so my standards are low."

Her house. I went to my computer and turned it on. It booted up normally, which was a relief. Now all I had to do was uninstall SimuLife.

"Whatcha doing?" Rina peered over my shoulder.

"Here's the thing," I said, casually trying to block her view of the screen. If I somehow figured out how to get rid of the game, would it, like, *kill* her? I assumed it would just send her back into the game, but I didn't want her thinking that I wished her any harm (even though I kind of did). "You don't happen to know how you got here, do you?"

"Nope! One second I was in my house—"

"In the game. SimuLife."

"Yeah, in my house, and all of a sudden *boom*, I was here!" Rina took a running jump onto the bed, bouncing onto it and then off it onto the floor. She squealed a barely suppressed "Whee!" Christ.

"Could you not do that in those heels?" I asked. "They were kind of expensive."

"Oh, sorry," Rina said, unbuckling the silver sandals. She chucked them onto a pile of crumpled jeans. I glared at her and got up to put them back on the shoe shelf in the closet. Then I went back to my computer and clicked the SimuLife icon. The "Welcome to SimuLife!" window popped up again, although this time my computer didn't freeze. Progress. Now that it was actually in front of me, I vaguely remembered playing it back in the day. Granted, it was for a few weeks, tops. There hadn't seemed to be much of a point other than making an avatar of yourself and having it do random things. I went over to "options" and selected "uninstall."

A message popped up: "Please insert game disk."

I sighed deeply. Maybe I could just delete everything in my account. I clicked "sign in."

"Please insert game disk," said the popup window again.

I clicked on "cancel account."

"Please insert game disk" said the popup window yet again.

Of course I didn't have the game disk. Of course it wasn't going to be that easy.

"So how was your day?" asked Rina, who was now sitting on the floor giving herself a pedicure with some of my nail polish. I walked over to my closet. It's a fairly big walk-in and there are some built-in cubbies along the back wall, where I usually throw tech stuff I don't need anymore—old cell phones, manuals, warranties, all that crap. I started digging around, wondering whether the old SimuLife disk was in there somewhere. I didn't know whether uninstalling the program was the way to go, or whether some other solution would reveal itself if I could just sign into the game. Either way, I needed that disk.

"My day," I said, tossing aside some dusty USB cables, "was extremely stressful. Probably because I spent all of it worrying about what to do about you and how to get rid of you—" Whoops.

"Get rid of me?" Rina sounded hurt.

"Yeah, well . . . I mean, no, not get rid of you. But you know, how do we put you back in the game?" I asked. "That's where you live. I'm sure you want to go back there, right?" I started sorting through a stack of random CDs. No SimuLife. I did find something marked "summer vacation sing-along mix," which looked promising and which I flung onto my bed, but no SimuLife.

"Not really." Rina shrugged. She admired her newly painted toes. They were now a pale, shimmery peach color, and I was surprised she hadn't picked one of the glittery fuchsias or bright greens in the polish collection. "All I do there is sit around the house. I write in my journal a lot, but there's never much to write about. Out here is way better. By the way, I went downstairs and ate some cookies because I was hungry. I hope that's okay."

"Oh my God, yeah," I said. "Sorry, I didn't realize—of course, yes, eat whatever you want. Are you still hungry? Do you want something else?" Wait a minute, what was I doing? I was trying to get rid of her, not running a bed-and-breakfast.

"No," Rina said, indicating an empty package of Oreos in the corner.

"Wow," I said. "Hope you have a fast metabolism."

"I do if you do," she answered cheerfully. "Oh! I almost forgot. Right before you got home someone called for you. Anne? I talked to her."

"*What*?!" I froze in the middle of shuffling through another stack of old CDs.

"Yeah, she wanted to know if you could forward her a physics e-mail your teacher sent that she accidentally deleted, so I said sure—"

"You pretended to be me? Are you *crazy?*"

"No, it was fun! So I thought tomorrow, I could go out and—"

"What? No! It's bad enough you picked up the phone, which you can't do anymore, by the way. And you definitely can't leave the house."

"Why not?"

"Rina. Think about it."

She thought—visibly. She actually looked like she was pondering a weighty dilemma. Then she looked totally bummed and I realized how I must've seemed to my friends all day.

"It might be weird if people saw two of us?" she asked.

"Yes! Thank you. And it would *definitely* be weird. I'm just glad you didn't talk to Anne long enough for her to think something was up." At least, I fervently hoped that was the case. Anne's round, angelic face concealed a penchant for casually messing with my head. It's generally a minor annoyance, and anyone who even noticed would've thought it was just teasing, but the last thing I needed was for Rina to provide her with more material. I opened a dusty cardboard box, fighting not to sneeze.

"I could go out in disguise," Rina offered. "I could dye my hair! What do you think we'd look like blond?" She looked at herself in the mirror on the inside of my closet door and started messing around with her hair, taking out the pigtails and putting it in different styles—a ponytail, a side ponytail, and a messy bun, before giving up and letting the waves hang loose.

"Terrible," I told her. "I tried it sophomore year and trust me, it doesn't work; our hair is too dark for it to actually look good, and it's not right for our skin tone."

Whoa, I'd just said "our hair" and "our skin tone" as if it were perfectly normal for someone else with my exact hair and skin tone to be sitting in the room with me. I shook my head and gave myself five minutes to finish looking for the disk. A giant, tangled pile of cords and cables later, I had searched my entire closet. Still no Simu-Life. Of course.

Fine, I'd buy a new one. Rina was now giving herself a rather messy manicure with the same color she'd used on her toes. I felt her pain; I can never paint my own nails without basically covering my entire fingertips with polish either. I took advantage of her silence to go back to the computer and google SimuLife. I scanned the results of the search. Online simulation game . . . never really got popular . . . discontinued three years ago. Okay, so much for going to the store and buying it. I trolled eBay. Nothing. I checked Craigslist. Nothing.

"All right, look," I said to Rina. She looked up. "The next couple weeks are really important to me. Like, *really* important. I've got finals, the SATs, my Yale visit *and* interview, and I still have to write my application essay, so . . . obviously you can stay here for now, but—"

"Yay! Thank you!" She made a move like she was going to jump up and hug me, but then realized she had a nail polish brush in her hand that was about to drip onto the carpet. She hastily put the brush back in the bottle.

"*But*," I continued, "you've gotta lie low, okay? I mean, obviously we're gonna have to do something about you eventually, but I just don't have time to deal with it right now. So we'll figure it out in a few weeks, okay?" I couldn't believe I was letting a virtual stranger move into my bedroom with me, but I couldn't think of another solution.

"Okay!" Rina said enthusiastically, waving her hands around to dry her nails.

A door opened downstairs. "Hello?" my mom called. Oh wow, she was home early.

"Hey Mom!" I yelled down, and then hissed at Rina, "Go in the closet."

"What?" she asked.

"Shhh! She's probably on her way upstairs, so—" We heard the stairs creak and I grabbed Rina by the elbow, shoved her into the closet, and closed the door.

"Hey," I said to my mom as she approached, amazing myself with how casual I sounded. I leaned back against the closet door, bracing my feet on the floor in case Rina did something stupid.

"Hey," she said, poking her head around the edge of my door frame. "I had a client dinner but she bailed because her kid got sick. Thank God, right? That she bailed, not the sick-kid thing." She took off her glasses and stashed them in her purse. "So . . . dinner?" she asked. "You and me? Are you okay just ordering something?"

"Aren't I always?" I asked, smiling.

"I raised my daughter right," she said, smiling back and reaching up to rub her neck with one hand, then slowly rolling her shoulders in a circle. "Okay, I'll tell you when it gets here. You go back to studying, or . . . cleaning. Good lord." She looked around at the complete and utter disaster that was my room, and I suppressed the urge to yell, "It wasn't me!"

I waited a few minutes after she left, then stuck my head inside my closet. Rina was sitting cross-legged on the floor and opened her mouth to say something. I quickly made a "shhhh" gesture with my finger.

"She wants me to come down for dinner. Just stay in here, okay?" I whispered. "You can use my computer or something but if you even hear one stair squeaking, you gotta go back in the closet." Rina nodded.

I closed the door on her, then went downstairs and plopped down on the living room couch, pondering whether "Mommy and Me: The Adventures of Two Single Ladies Who Both Suck at Cooking" would be a good essay idea. Hmm, maybe. I jotted it down on a Post-it, then opened my AP Euro book, psyched to be away from Rina for a bit. Worst-case scenario, she would just have to . . . what? She

couldn't move in permanently. I couldn't kick her out in the
street, or send her to a homeless shelter, or stick her in the
state foster care system.

I was gonna have to figure this out somehow.

Just not right now.

MORE THINGS TO DO

- Anything Paul asks
- Figure out how to get rid of clone
- Attempt not to go insaner
- Essay!!!

CHAPTER SEVEN
WEDNESDAY, DECEMBER 5

THE NEXT MORNING IN THE MIDDLE OF EURO,
Kyla leaned over and wrote, "Long lunch?" on my notebook. That's Kyla-speak for ditching fifth period and
going to the mall. I started to write back to her, but she
flicked my pen aside and wrote, "Let me guess. No. Too
much work."

I smiled ruefully and nodded. She rolled her eyes at
me and wrote, "Sucks to be you!" I managed to scribble,
"Thanks," before we both got the feeling we were missing
too much of the French Revolution lecture currently being
spewed forth at the front of the room.

Before lunch Kyla dangled her car keys in my face with
her "one last chance!" look, but I waved her off as Anne
walked up to me.

"Hey, thanks for forwarding me that physics e-mail,"
she said, fiddling with the end of her blond ponytail. "I can't

believe you were already home when I called yesterday. I figured I would just leave you a message."

I smiled and nodded at her, my fingers clenching slightly as I imagined strangling Rina. "Yeah, I was kinda speeding," I said casually.

"You sounded a little weird on the phone, though. Are you okay?"

"I'm fine, I just had a bad headache yesterday," I explained, willing myself not to panic. *She doesn't know anything. She couldn't possibly know anything! She's just making conversation.* I shook my head when Anne asked if I was coming to lunch, not relishing the thought of sitting down at a table with her, even with a bunch of our other friends. Instead, I bypassed the cafeteria altogether and dragged Paul to the yearbook office with me.

"Hooking up on school grounds is your way of making up for practice yesterday, huh?" he asked, grinning as I pulled him inside and shut the door.

"Shut up," I said, chucking my bag onto the table in the middle of the room and sinking into a chair. The yearbook office is actually just a conference room inside the library, but the door is really thick, so you can make as much noise as you want. "This is me spending quality time with my boyfriend while also getting work done. Are you in or out?"

"I'm in," Paul said, leaning over to give me a quick kiss. "It's far better for me to sit here and silently watch you work than go back to the cafeteria, where people are actually having fun." I shot him a warning look and he grinned. "Kidding, of course." He sat down across from me and started eating, while I took out my laptop and opened up a blank document. The mom essay from last night had, predictably, fizzled out after half a page, so once again I was searching for a topic.

"Losing the State Volleyball Championship on a Technicality Thanks to the Asshat of a Referee"?

"Academic Camp: Not Just for Nerds, Even Though I Was Pretty Nerdy the Summer Between Seventh and Eighth Grades"?

"Marching Band Requires Too Much Talent and an Interest in Marching"?

No, no, and no. I then semiseriously considered writing about a certain mishap involving Paul's lips, my lips, and his allergy to one of my lip glosses, but there's a line between uniquely quirky and glaringly inappropriate, and the line isn't even that fine. So I nixed that one.

After the last bell of the day rang, I was at my locker putting my stuff in my book bag when Kyla sprinted up behind me and smacked me between the shoulder blades.

"You lying bitch!" she said very close to my head, just as I was shutting my locker door. I turned around and saw her staring at me, looking annoyed. She was wearing a minuscule Catholic schoolgirl skirt and angrily yanking the zipper of her little green ski jacket up and down.

"Yup, I'm a prevaricating . . . um . . . bitch," I said, failing to come up with a synonym for bitch except for the one about seeing somebody next Tuesday, and I certainly wasn't going to use that. Kyla glared at me, the look on her face a mixture of anger and triumph. "All right, what'd I do?" I asked.

Kyla folded her arms. "You fully went to the mall at lunch, you sneaky little liar. You undercover slacker, I may never trust you again!"

"What?" I laughed. "No I didn't." I'd only taken Kyla up on a long lunch once in my entire high school career, and it certainly hadn't been anytime near finals.

"Yes, you did," she said.

"Kyla, I was in the yearbook office doing work. Do you want to see the files on my laptop?" I let my bag slide off my shoulder so that I could reach the zipper, in case she actually did want to see.

Kyla shook her head impatiently, her red hair coming loose from its haphazard bobby-pinning. She stuck out her bottom lip and blew the strands off her face. "I totally saw you. I yelled at you, but I guess you were too far away to hear. You were coming out of Hot Topic with a huge bag."

"Okay, Hot Topic? It *clearly* wasn't me." Seriously?

Maybe I wasn't the only one having hallucinations lately. Unless—

Oh no.

No!

I gulped, struggling not to pass out from horror.

"Okay, well—I mean, whoever it was looked exactly like you, then," Kyla said, still sounding doubtful. "And the thing was, she was wearing a shirt that looked just like that really baggy, ratty flannel one you always—"

"What?" I practically shrieked. Oh, *hell* no! Not only did Rina leave the house and go to the mall, she had evidently stolen my grandfather's favorite shirt. Not okay. So not okay.

Kyla gave me a weird look and took a step back. "So . . . was that you or wasn't it?"

"It was totally not me," I said quickly. "I was here."

Kyla looked me up and down. "Yeah, I guess if it *were* you, why would you go home and change first?" I was in the same outfit I'd been wearing all day—jeans and a short-sleeved green tee layered over a long-sleeved brown one—plus my button-up red winter coat. "Sorry, I totally suck," Kyla said, still looking perplexed, but also apologetic. "Watch out, though. You might have an evil twin running around the mall." She elbowed me and grinned. I'm pretty sure I went totally pale at that thought, but I managed to scrounge up a smile.

"Well," I said, "If I run into her I'll make sure to kick her ass." In my head, there was no "if" in that sentence. It was more like, "I'm about to run home and *definitely* kick her ass."

"That's the spirit!" said Kyla, playing with the zipper on her jacket again. "All right, go home. I know you're *dying* to study some more SAT words or whatever the hell." She took off down the hallway as I pictured a thousand different methods of killing Rina. I then sped all the way home, to get the killing started as soon as possible.

"Hi!" Rina said when I walked in. She was lying on my bed, reading *The Swiss Family Robinson*. She must have finished the thesaurus. "How was your day?"

I stared at her. There was a crumpled-up Hot Topic bag on the floor and she was wearing skintight purple and black zebra-patterned jeans, a black tank top with the word HARLOT written on the front in some sort of red-sequined pointy devil font, skull-and-crossbones bracelets, and what looked like a dog collar around her neck.

"How was my day?" I asked her. "HOW WAS MY DAY? How the hell do you think my day was? My friend Kyla saw you at the mall! And now she thinks I'm a bitch *and* that I dress like a baby goth ho!"

Rina looked down at her outfit. "I know, right? It's so cute. I figured I would get away from all the pink, so—"

"Did you not hear what I just said?!" I have never even

come close to starting a girlfight, at least not since preschool, but I wanted very badly to grab Rina by the hair and slam her face into the wall. Repeatedly.

Rina saw my expression, and her smile disappeared. "I'm sorry," she said, chucking her book aside and sitting up straight. "It's just—I know I wasn't supposed to leave your room, but I was just so bored, and I got the bus schedule off the Internet and you had a ton of change in your piggy bank. . . ." I stared at her and she started talking faster. "I'm sorry. Please don't be mad. Don't you like our new clothes?"

"*No,*" I said, recoiling in disgust as I stared at her outfit again. She'd bought a *lot* of stuff. I looked over at my piggy bank, which was lying on the floor. "How much money did I have in there, exactly?"

"Oh, it was mostly change, but there were some twenties. You must've shoved 'em in at some point and forgotten about them," Rina said. Her brief foray into remorse was evidently already over and she seemed all cheerful again. Great.

I sighed and flopped down on the bed. "Rina," I said, forcing a note of patience into my voice, "you can't just go wherever you want. I mean, you've already been spotted. That can't happen again. Okay?"

"I guess," she said, scooching over on the bed to make more room for me. "But couldn't we just tell people we're twins?"

"But we're not!" I exclaimed, sitting up. "I've lived here my whole life. People know I'm an only child! It's not like we're long-lost—here, give me your hand." She held it out and I yanked her toward me, then held both of our hands up to the light. "Okay, if we're twins, we'll still have different fingerprints. Right? They're like snowflakes. So let's see if . . ." I squinted at her fingers, then my own, then nodded in resignation. It wasn't hard to tell that the ridges and whorls on her fingertips were the exact same as the ones on mine; not just similar, but exactly the same. "See?" I said. "If somebody found out about you, they'd probably throw us into a government testing facility or something. They'd dissect us in a lab. I don't wanna be dissected in a lab, thanks very much. I kinda like my parts where they are."

I flopped back down on the bed. "This is so the last thing I need right now."

"Yeah, you look stressed," Rina agreed.

"Thanks," I said sarcastically. "You aren't exactly helping by gallivanting around town. And you would be stressed too if you had to retake the SATs in less than two weeks, but before that there were finals, and . . ." I rattled off my "life sucks because" list that I usually confine to my most private neurotic moments, and she had the decency to look appropriately worried for a split second before jumping in and reciting the end of the list along with me. Smart-ass.

"By the way, is it really hot in here or is it just me?" I asked.

"Oh, I turned the heat up," Rina said. I looked at her and rolled my eyes.

"What?" she asked. "I know Mom turns the heat off when you guys aren't here, but I was here."

"Quit calling her Mom. And you weren't here, you were at the mall."

She shrugged. "Not the whole day."

My eyes widened and I snapped my head around to look at her. "Oh my God, did you go anywhere else?"

"No, I came straight back. Calm down." Rina actually sounded a little impatient. Since when was *I* annoying *her*?

"Oh, now my cybertwin is telling me to calm down. Great." I sat down at the computer and started checking my e-mail.

"You don't understand," said Rina, sitting back down on the bed. "Do you know how *boring* it was being in that game for the last four years? Hello! You didn't even put that much stuff in my house! Thank God you remembered the TV! And now you just want me to stay in your room all day? It's almost worse! It *is* worse!"

"Fine," I said, deleting a few e-mail messages and then sending myself a reminder to get new number two pencils. "Tomorrow you can leave my room. Watch TV. Go anywhere in the house you want. Just don't *leave*, okay?"

"Really?" Rina's eyes widened enthusiastically. "Cool! Thanks."

"You're welcome," I said, relieved that she'd gone along so easily. "Now if you don't mind, I have a lot of work to do." I closed my e-mail and opened up a word document, on the very off chance that essay inspiration suddenly struck.

"No problem! I'm gonna finish this book," Rina said, picking up *The Swiss Family Robinson* again. "Once I'm done, though, do you have any recommendations?"

I looked toward my bookshelf and its row of all seven Harry Potter hardcovers. "Yeah," I said, jerking my head toward them. "Those."

"Wow, those will take me a while."

"That's the idea." I put on my headphones, turned to the computer, and grabbed my physics textbook to work on robot calculations. I could hear Rina through the music, but the one time she asked, "Hey Kate?" I pretended I couldn't.

There's only so much a girl can take.

Dear Diary,

Yay, Kate's letting me leave her room! She won't let me go outside yet, but I'm sure I'll be able to convince her soon. At least, I hope so. Because the mall was way fun yesterday, and I don't want to end up stuck in here and getting all bored like I was at home. I want to do stuff! I want to meet people! I don't want to just watch TV all day again, and I *definitely* don't want to have to kill time by writing a bazillion journal entries. Oh my God, see, I'm already doing it! Aaaaah, I have to stop!

I'd so rather be at the mall. Or at school. Or in the backyard. Or anywhere.

At least Kate has lots of books I can read. So does her mom, although most of hers seem to be about sexy pirates.

Love, Rina

CHAPTER EIGHT
THURSDAY, DECEMBER 6

"WELL, HELLO THERE," PAUL SAID JUST AFTER second period. I had tracked him down at his locker, sneaked up behind him, and given him a huge hug. He squeezed me crushingly and then pulled me into a side hallway, away from the crowd of students rushing off to their next class. "Didn't see much of you yesterday."

"Aw, I know," I said, my arms around his waist. I snuggled my face into his shoulder, despite the slightly scratchy surface of his gray wool sweater. Behind him, someone came around the corner, said, "Get a goddamn room," and then turned around and left.

"We refuse," I called down the hallway. "We only hook up in public. It's our thing." Paul laughed, and he was about to bend his head to kiss me when I was distracted by my phone beeping. I checked the text. It was from Josh, one of the assistant editors on the paper, asking if I could help him with some quick ad layouts after school. "Ugh," I said, then texted back, OK. If I didn't help him today, I'd probably just have to fix whatever he messed up later.

"So, no practice again today, huh?" Paul said. He'd been reading my phone over my shoulder, and he raised an eyebrow at me.

I looked up at him, confused for a second, and then my eyes widened as I realized that I'd just blown off his basketball practice again, right before his very eyes. I opened my mouth to apologize, but he cut me off.

"You know what, don't worry about it. It actually reminds me that I can't go shopping with you tomorrow."

"Aww!" I said, even as half of my brain went, "YES!" We'd planned a quick Christmas shopping jaunt weeks ago and I'd budgeted a few hours on Friday afternoon for it, but I could actually really use that time for other things.

"Yeah," Paul continued, "my dad set up this last-minute meeting with some Yale board member, so . . . sorry." He made a cute frowny face at me.

"Well, it gives me more time to study and that's always a plus." I shrugged and reached up to fix his hair.

"Hey, don't sound *too* disappointed," Paul said, ducking his head away. His voice was half-playful, half . . . not. "It sounds like if I hadn't canceled, you would've."

"Oh, come on," I said. He couldn't be mad at *me* about this, could he? "You know I'd rather go with you. But if you can't do it, then I have a couple extra hours to work, which I could use this week."

Paul nodded a little and his face softened. "Yeah, I know. Well, do you need help? I'll be your study buddy if you want," he offered. "And if that's the only time I can see you," he added, playing with a lock of my hair.

"You're nice." I smiled back. "Maybe a few hours on Sunday?"

"Yes, and if we accidentally get naked some time during said study session, that'll just be—"

I punched him in the arm.

"—awful, and we'd put our clothes back on and go right back to hitting the books," he finished. He gave me a quick kiss as I giggled. Then I watched, amused, as two freshman girls openly admired him as he walked away down the hall.

My interaction with the other guy in my life was not quite as pleasant. As soon as I sat down in physics, Jake threw a folder at me. It skidded across the table and sliced a paper cut onto my pinky finger. "Ow!" I yelped, and jumped back.

"Yikes," he said. "Sorry."

I waved my hand around, then looked at the cut, which had turned into a thin red line with two tiny blood droplets. "Thanks," I said. "Appreciate it. Love being mortally wounded as soon as I walk into class." I went over to the fat roll of brown paper towel sitting on the counter along the classroom's back wall and ripped off a piece to dab my finger.

"It's just a paper cut," Jake said, glancing casually at my hand and then hopefully toward the clock, as if he thought class might be over already.

"It's a folder cut," I corrected. "It's much worse."

"It's a little worse," he said.

"Well, it's not good either way." I waved my hand around some more, waiting for the stinging to go away.

"Let me see," he said. He grabbed my wrist and pulled me closer to get a better look at the cut. I rolled my eyes and let him, then realized that Anne was looking at us from across the room, eyebrows raised, clearly registering that Jake was holding my hand in his. I quickly backed away, my chair scraping across the floor.

Jake shrugged. "Well, I'm sorry all my hard work almost defingered you, but . . ." He opened the folder he'd thrown at me and showed off several neat pages of calculations. "You have to admit this looks pretty good."

"Oh," I said, pulling the folder over and scanning the rows of numbers. I didn't even bother to hide the utter shock in my voice. "Wow. Yeah."

"Hey, I wasn't gonna let you flunk. I mean, how can you flounce off to your Ivy League school of choice if you flunk?" Jake gave me an innocent, wide-eyed look.

"I was thinking more of a sashay, not a flounce, but thanks." I took out a pencil and started comparing his numbers to the ones I'd done on my half of the lab. They all checked out.

"How are those college apps going, anyway?" he asked. Around us, the room buzzed with conversation and random pings and clanks, plus the occasional swear word, as everyone else worked busily. I noticed Anne glancing in our direction again, but now that she had nothing to see but me and Jake talking, she begrudgingly went back to her own project.

I looked at Jake, surprised. "You actually want to know?"

"Not really, but if you say they're going terribly, I can figure out a way to make fun of you. And if you say they're going great, I can also figure out a way to make fun of you. So it's sort of a win-win question for me."

I gave him a tight little smile. "Heh. Hilarious. They're going fine, thank you. Or at least they will be once I figure out what the hell I should write my essay about."

"Oh, I'm sure you'll think of something." Jake yawned and stretched his arms over his head. "Let's see, you could talk about how you've learned that rules are not, in fact, meant to be broken," he suggested, picking a pencil-size tube of metal from our robot supply box and flipping it through his long, thin fingers. "Or wait, maybe you should write about the one time you actually"—he paused to mock-gasp—"colored outside the lines. Oh, wait, no, you don't do that anymore."

I reached into his bag, pulled out a marker, and used it to color several large sloppy patches of red on the pages of his open physics textbook.

"Okay," he said, pulling the book away from me and looking down at the now-splotchy pages 176 and 177. "Well, good for you. I guess that's your essay topic right there."

"I'm actually thinking something about how my lab partner is a huge pain in the ass." I took out my calculator, then sighed. "All right, what the hell are we doing here?"

Jake shrugged, then scooched his chair back and put his feet up on the table. "You're the smart one—why don't you tell me?"

I gingerly picked up one of the robot arms that we'd started putting together yesterday. It immediately fell apart in my hands.

"You just killed our robot. Guess you're not the smart one after all." Jake sighed dramatically.

"I'm going to answer that by throwing this at your head," I said, grabbing one of the Ping-Pong balls out of our supply box. And I did.

After the last bell of the day rang, I took out my phone

to turn the sound back on and noticed a text from my mom. The text said, **Are you sick? Call me.** Weird.

I called her back. "Hey Mom, no, I'm not sick, I'm just leaving school now." I headed for the parking lot, shifting my bag to my other shoulder and almost dropping my phone in the process.

"Oh, okay," my mom said, "because Marta, you know, next door called, and . . ." Dammit. I already knew where this was going. Our next-door neighbor is a retired college professor and she's home most of the time. She must've seen Rina. Which meant that Rina left the house.

"It must've been someone else," I said flatly, making a beeline to my car and a plan to wring Rina's neck. "I've been at school all day," I continued. "You can call the attendance office and ask for my record if you want."

"I believe you, honey," my mom said. "You don't have to sound so defensive."

"I'm not being defensive!" Except that I was totally being defensive. Paranoia and panic tend to do that to you, and fury doesn't exactly help you cover it up. I reached my car door and started a one-handed search through my bag for my car keys, finding lip gloss, a crumpled-up to-do list, and three pens first. I swore under my breath before finally closing my fingers around my scratched-up mini-flashlight key chain.

"Okay, well, I just wanted to check," my mom said. "Marta's getting pretty old," she added, laughing a little. "I guess she made a mistake."

"Yeah," I agreed.

But Rina had made a bigger one.

CHAPTER NINE

"ALL RIGHT," I DECLARED. "HERE'S HOW IT'S gonna be."

"Okay," Rina said. She didn't sound happy, but she also seemed resigned. It was late that night, and we were both sitting on the floor in my room, leaning back against the side of my bed. What had started as me screaming at her as soon as I walked in had fizzled when she swore to me that she hadn't left the house. Apparently, my neighbor had seen her through the window and while Rina probably should have closed the living room curtains before plunking down to watch TV, she hadn't technically gone anywhere. So I couldn't *really* be mad at her.

But I still was.

"One," I said. "Only one of us can leave the house at a time. End of story. If I'm at school or wherever, you're in here. Curtains closed."

Rina nodded, then continued plowing through the chicken-flavored cup o'noodles I'd brought up for her. For good measure I got out a yellow legal pad and started writing the rules down.

"Two," I continued. "This doesn't mean you can never leave." Rina immediately brightened, but I refused to smile back at her and instead kept going. "I know it sucks to be inside twenty-four seven, so it's probably okay for you to go running every once in a while and just pretend to be me. So if you wanna do that, fine, just let me know first, and I'll stay in here. You can borrow my workout clothes."

"Aaaaaghh!!! Thank you!" Rina leaned toward me like she was going to give me a hug, but I frantically waved her off. "Quiet! My mom's sleeping!"

"Sorry," Rina whispered. She went back to eating her noodles.

"Three. When we're both at home, one of us stays in this room. Four. When we're both in this room, one of us stays in the closet."

"We're breaking that one right now," she pointed out.

"I know," I said impatiently, "because my mom's asleep, but the second we hear her door open . . ." We both cocked our heads to listen, suddenly paranoid. Rina scooted toward the closet so that she was sitting half inside it and half out.

"And rule number five," I said finally, after a few more moments of listening to see if my mom had woken up. "You will not be having any contact with anybody I know, including my friends and most especially my boyfriend."

Rina's eyes practically bugged out of her head. "You have a boyfriend?" she squealed.

"Yes," I said. "His name is Paul, and you can go ahead and focus on the part about you not having any contact with him."

"Is he hot?" she demanded. She was done with her noodles now and set the foam cup and spoon off to the side, staring at me eagerly.

I rolled my eyes a little, but couldn't help smiling. "Completely irrelevant, but yes, he's hot. He's like six three, brown hair a little lighter than ours, blue eyes. . . ."

"Do you have pictures?"

"Of course." I went over to the dresser and picked up my phone, then noticed the little text icon on the screen. A message must've come in and I hadn't heard it. "Hang on a sec," I said, checking the text. It was from Josh and it was hours old. All it said was **hey where are u?** I sighed and very nearly slapped myself on the forehead, suddenly remembering my promise to help him with ad layout after school. **Sorry** I typed back, my face flushing slightly with embarrassment at forgetting even though I was in my own house. **Didn't get this till now. Something came up, will help u tomorrow at lunch ok?** I closed my phone, mentally reshuffled my schedule since I had been planning on studying for my government final during lunch, then went over to the computer and e-mailed myself a reminder to go to the newspaper office instead. I found a few pictures of Paul and handed the phone to Rina so she could take a look.

Her eyes widened as she clicked through the photos, some of Paul, some of Paul and me together. "Niiice," she said, squeaking in approval. She held out her hand for a high five.

"Thank you," I said. I high-fived her and smiled.

"Man," she continued wistfully, now scrolling through random pics on my cell, including some candids of me and Kyla goofing around in the hallway at school, and a few posed pictures of a bunch of us all dressed up for homecoming a few months ago. "Your life out here is so exciting."

"Uh, no." I sat back down and leaned against the bed, stretching my legs out in front of me. "Trust me, if it were that exciting I'd already have something to write my personal statement about."

"This looks pretty exciting," she said dryly, extending the phone toward me. It was a picture from last August of Paul doing a body shot off my stomach.

"Yeah, well, I can't exactly write my essay about that, can I?" Hmmm. Or maybe I could?

"Well, either way," said Rina, "I'd totally rather be swamped with finals and the SATs and all that stuff, as long as I got to go to school and hang out with my friends, and the hot boyfriend is just a bonus. A *huge* bonus!" Her whole face lit up, and it was almost cute how much she clearly, genuinely, thought my life was awesome.

I couldn't help but laugh a little. "Yeah, that part's not bad, I'll admit."

"And it's way, way better than just sitting around the house with nothing to do for four years."

"Oh come on," I said, nudging her with my foot. "Is that really what happened?"

"Of course. What the hell did you think happened?" she asked. "You didn't even give me a car."

"I was in eighth grade—I couldn't drive," I explained. "I mean, I only played that game for a few weeks. It got really boring really fast, no offense."

"None taken," Rina said. "Anyway, you were the one in charge. You could've made it exciting if you wanted. But instead you just . . . bailed." Her voice had gone soft, and she pulled her legs up with her arms and rested her chin on her knees, her eyes toward the floor.

"I didn't bail," I said defensively. "Well, I did, but it's not like I knew you were, like, *alive* in there."

"I know, but still. I was. And you just left me all by myself. I didn't have anything to do. I didn't even have anything to read—you didn't put any books in my house." Rina didn't sound angry, just resigned, and as I looked at her bummed-out face I was suddenly overwhelmed with guilt.

"I'm sorry, I guess I just . . . didn't really know what the deal was," I said lamely.

"Yeah, well, that's what it was," she answered. "Thanks for giving me a TV, at least. Although a DVR would've been nice. A lot of shows are on at the same time."

I stared at her, horrified. I'd never thought about it this way before. Why would I? It was a *game*. But I'd clearly screwed Rina over, and now I was doing it again, trapping her in the jail cell of my bedroom. My face went somber, mirroring the expression on hers, but after a few seconds she seemed to shake off her gloom. She shook her head, flipping her hair around a little. "So what's the story with all these people?" Rina asked. She picked up my phone again and took another scroll through the pictures. "Tell me about them." Her voice was back to its normal cheeriness now, and she sounded eager and curious.

I grinned and rolled my eyes. "Oh, man, do you have a while?"

"Um, yeah," she answered, in a very "duh" tone.

"Oh, right," I said. "Well, I have to do another two practice sections and work on my essay a little. But I'll tell you a few stories when I'm done, okay? You good with the Harry Potter till then?"

"Sure," she said. "Or, oooh, actually, do you have more pictures?"

"Yep," I said, getting up and gesturing for her to follow

me over to my computer. I clicked open my pictures folder. "Here, go nuts."

"Awesome," Rina said, already staring wide-eyed at all my photos. They were mainly of Paul and my friends, and most of them were from the past couple years, but there were some baby pics and some of my mom in there as well. Rina couldn't help squealing at practically every new photo she clicked on—"Oooh, you're at the beach!" "Oooh, Halloween!" "Oooh, look at that hat!"—and I smiled. "Glad you like 'em, but keep it down a little, okay? You're going to wake up my—"

We suddenly heard my mother's door open and then the sound of her footsteps coming down the hallway. In a flash, Rina vaulted over the bed and retreated into the closet, and I sat down at my computer just as Mom stuck her head in the door.

"Sorry, was I being too noisy?" I asked, leaning casually back in my computer chair and giving her an innocent look. "I was just on the phone with Kyla." I suddenly realized my phone was over on the floor by the closet, and I prayed my mom didn't notice how far away it was from where I was sitting.

"This late?" she asked, stepping inside a little and leaning against the door frame. I shrugged and nodded. "No, I just wanted to get some water and decided to check in on you," she said. "How's the essay going?"

I made a sort of "eeeeuughhhh" noise and she smiled. "Well, I'm sure it'll turn out great. Night, honey."

"Night, Mom." She closed the door behind her. After five full minutes, Rina cracked open the closet door and peeked out.

"Coast clear," I said, still feeling a little paranoid. That had been waaaay too close.

"Cool." She came out and went back to looking at the photos on my computer as I gathered up my SAT practice book, a notebook, and some pens and pencils.

"What's going on with Kyla and these four guys?" Rina asked, indicating a picture of Kyla in a green flapper dress being held horizontally in the air by four of our guy friends, as Paul stood off to the side, half out of frame, cracking up, and our other friend Sam blurrily ran through the back of the shot with a feather boa wrapped around his head.

I laughed. "Oh, that. That . . . was an incident at our homecoming after-party. I'll tell you all about it when I get back upstairs." I headed for the door.

"Aw, come on!" Rina pleaded.

"Suck it up and wait till I'm done with all my work." I suddenly thought of something. "Actually, you know what? Suck it up and wait till tomorrow after school."

"What? No, don't make me wait till then!"

"No, I think you'll like this," I said. I had suddenly realized how I could make up for Rina's four years of utter boredom inside SimuLife—well, for a tiny fraction of it, anyway. "I'm taking you shopping." Paul might have canceled, but there was no reason I couldn't go anyway. I still needed to get Christmas shopping done, after all. More important, after hearing how Rina had spent the last four years doing nothing, I wanted to take her outside.

Rina's eyes practically bugged out of her head. She opened her mouth, was too overjoyed to actually say anything, and instead did a series of enthusiastic fingertip claps.

"Shopping!" she finally whispered. "Together, though? What about rule number one?"

"We're breaking it," I said. "Just this once. Because you cannot keep dressing like that," I added, eyeing the black short shorts with a silver cat logo she was wearing. Probably another Hot Topic find. The cat logo itself even looked slutty somehow.

"Does that mean you're going to choose clothes for me tomorrow?" Rina asked.

"No, I'm going to choose clothes for me," I said. "But you can wear them if you want."

Rina shrieked with joy, then realized she'd shrieked and immediately retreated into the closet. She stayed there until I left for school the next day.

Dear Diary,

I. Am. Soooo excited to go shopping! Kate already said she mostly wants to get Christmas presents—she's got a whole list with everyone she knows on it (she tries to be very, very organized). But hopefully we'll also have time to get clothes for ourselves. After all, she deserves it—she works way too hard.

And I deserve it too! ☺

The only bummer is that Kate thinks my taste in clothes sucks. But I've been studying her style and you know what her style is? Boring.

Don't tell her I said that. ☺

Love, Rina

CHAPTER TEN
FRIDAY, DECEMBER 7

"WHERE ARE WE GOING?" ASKED RINA BREATH- lessly as she got in my car the next day after school. She was wearing one of my old winter coats, an orange scarf, some very raggedy mittens, and some purple earmuffs that I'd probably last looked at in the sixth grade.

I reached over and plucked the earmuffs off her head. "Nope," I said, chucking them into the backseat and then backing out of the driveway.

"But they're such a cute color!" She turned around and looked at them wistfully, then sighed. "So where are we going?"

"The outlets," I answered, and her eyes grew wide.

"Outlet shopping? *Outlet shopping*? Eeeeeeeeeeee!!!!!" That was actually the sound that came out of her mouth, and it was extremely loud and extremely high-pitched. I rolled my eyes a little, but couldn't help smiling at her giddiness.

"Yeah, well, my money goes further at the outlets," I said. "Plus, they're almost an hour away, so the odds of us running into anybody are small." At least, I hoped they were. I had briefly considered making Rina wear giant sunglasses the whole time, but that seemed a little ridiculous given that it was the middle of winter and we were mostly going to be indoors.

"What stores are at the outlets?" Rina asked.

"Oh, I don't know, the usual," I answered, trying to remember as I sped up the on-ramp and merged onto the highway. "Coach." Rina squealed. "Banana Republic." Rina squealed. I visualized the outlet parking lot and the signs I always saw upon driving in. "Old Navy, um, J. Crew, some underwear store, a bunch of shoe stores . . ."

Rina threw her arms around my neck. "Thank you thank you thank you so much for taking me!" she screamed in my ear.

I quickly leaned my head away to preserve my hearing and almost bonked it right into the driver's side window. "You're welcome," I said, gunning into the right lane. "And now, in return . . ." I sighed and indicated my book bag in the backseat. "Can you grab my French grammar flash cards out of that and quiz me? I may have mentioned yesterday that this has to be a working drive."

"Oh, yeah, totally," Rina said. I gave her credit for not looking bummed out, since her hand had been in the air on its way to the CD player, and I knew she would've preferred to pump up the *Guys and Dolls* sound track and sing along all the way there. I knew that because I would've wanted to, too. But finals called.

It was getting dark by the time we pulled into the extremely crowded parking lot, even though it wasn't even four o'clock yet. "Where to first?" asked Rina, after another attempt to put on my old purple earmuffs and another forceful removal by me. I looked around.

"I don't know," I said. "I need to go to Coach for my mom and get a sweater or something for Paul, but other than that, you lead the way."

"Awesome! I wanna try on so many clothes!" Rina squealed.

She then headed straight for the Pepperidge Farm store.

A bag and a half of mint Milanos later, we finally made it to Coach, where I got my mom the cute silver wallet she'd told me months ago she wanted. After that, I got Paul a dark blue cashmere sweater at J. Crew, which I figured he would enjoy about a tenth as much as the rest of his present (Celtics tickets), but that I would very much enjoy seeing him wear.

"Hey," Rina said as I was paying for the sweater. "Can you come see these clothes?"

"Yep, one second," I answered, as the cashier, a sleepy-looking college guy, handed me back my change and receipt.

"Cool, twins," he said lazily. "That's kinda sexy."

We both smiled at him—Rina cheerfully, me sarcastically—as she dragged me away to the fitting room. She'd piled four different dresses, five pairs of jeans, and a few ruffly little tops on the bench inside. I moved them over, sat down, and started digging through my bag for a pen and my beat-up copy of *The Sound and the Fury*.

Rina seemed taken aback. "You're going to study?" she asked, kicking her shoes off. "Don't you want to try on clothes?"

"Of course I'm going to study," I said. "And as long as you try things on, it's the same difference, right?"

"Oh my God, right!" Rina exclaimed. She immediately started changing into one of the dresses as I got out some colored sticky tabs and started making notes in my book for the English take-home final due Monday. I didn't even look up as she methodically went through her stack, hangers occasionally clattering to the floor. When she found something that she liked, she told me to look up, and I'd glance into the mirror and see, well, myself, in a different outfit. We ended up leaving J. Crew empty-handed—not enough was on sale—but repeated our system all over the mall.

"Eh," I said to a black and white polka-dotted halter dress at Ann Taylor—the neckline was a little low. Actually, a lot low. I could've bought it for Kyla.

"Maybe," I said to a dove gray cardigan at Banana Republic. It was clearly very comfortable, and would go with a lot of stuff I already owned, but the ribbons at the neck and hem made it a little "librarian" for me.

"Hell yes," I said to the cute little red-and-beige faux-leather sneakers at a random shoe store. Mostly because they cost twelve bucks. Rina grinned and put her own shoes back on, and I stuck a bookmark in *The Sound and the Fury* and followed her to the counter. I happily handed her my wallet, psyched that I'd discovered how to shop while simultaneously doing work. *This* was time management—I felt more relaxed than I had in ages. Plus, Rina seemed overjoyed, and she was a quick study—she was now totally avoiding anything pink or skanky or goth, and pointing at stuff like fitted dark red cords and cute little black platform Mary Janes. By the time we were on the last store, she was only trying on things that I would have chosen myself.

"Congrats," I said to her, looking at the ribbed black tank top, cropped gray jacket, and low-waisted trouser-cut jeans she was checking out in the dressing room mirror. "You look great."

"Yay!" she said. "And that means you would too!"

I smiled and inspected the outfit again, making a mental note that I should wear it the next time Paul and I went out, and I couldn't help but stare at Rina in the mirror. It was weird and cool at the same time—looking at her was like looking at me. Except that Rina was having a better hair day.

We were just leaving the food court to head home, cinnamon pretzels and multiple shopping bags in hand, when Rina elbowed me. "Did you notice people are staring at us?"

"Of course they are," I said. "Look at what you're wearing." After I'd nixed her earmuffs in the car, she'd decided to wear her scarf as a headband—her extremely woolly, fluffy, fringed orange scarf. But she did have a point—as we were walking, I caught a few randoms giving us slightly longer than usual glances, and as we passed by a mirrored window, I did a double take as well.

"Okay," I admitted, "I see what you mean. But I guess I sometimes check out twins in public too." As if on cue, a little kid stopped dead in his tracks on the sidewalk and pointed at us. "Look, Mommy, twins!" he yelled.

"Shhh," his mom said, reaching out and pushing down his pointing hand. She looked at me and Rina apologetically, and we smiled at her. The kid was super cute, after all. Rina waved at him. He waved back. After a second, I waved at him too, and he smiled at us broadly, waggling both his mitten-clad hands back and forth so quickly they were a blur. Rina and I looked at each other and giggled.

And then I froze. Because several feet past the little kid stood Anne Conroy.

Uh-oh.

My heart constricted and I instantly stopped waving. I wasn't a *hundred* percent sure it was her, but whoever it was was heading directly toward us, her high, tight blond ponytail swinging above the wide collar of her blue and green coat. I stepped behind a lamppost, but even if I had been thin enough to fully fit behind it, that wasn't going to help. "Rina," I said in a low voice. "Run."

"What?" she asked.

"Run," I repeated. "Toward the car. Go! Now." She looked at me and then, without asking any more questions, she took off at a sprint. Which, in a crowd of holiday shoppers at an outlet mall, actually attracts more attention than if we'd just casually wandered off. *Great. Good call, me.* The girl who was probably Anne whipped her head in our direction a little weirdly, as did about five other people. Panicking, I ran too.

At first I took off in the same direction as Rina. Then I realized that getting closer to her was the exact opposite of what I wanted, so I abruptly turned around. I took a deliberately large loop around a corner of the parking lot, nearly getting hit by a minivan, then turned back toward my car, struggling to get my keys out of my bag. I'd just slid behind the steering wheel when Rina appeared out of the dark, her breath puffing in the frosty air. She ran full speed at the passenger-side door and just barely stopped herself from slamming face-first into it.

"Go, go, go!" I yelled, unlocking the door at the same time as she tried to pull the handle, which screwed us both up. We tried again twice before we finally managed to un-sync enough for it to work. She got in and chucked her bags in the backseat, and I peeled out of the parking lot.

"What the hell was that?" Rina asked, fighting to get her breath back as she put her seat belt on.

"I thought . . . I thought I saw someone I knew," I said, heading toward the highway. Luckily traffic was light, as I was in no state to navigate any bumper-to-bumper.

"Oh my God! Who?" Rina actually looked as scared as I felt. Maybe all my talk about us being thrown into a government testing facility had finally gotten through to her.

"My friend Anne, although I'm not totally sure it was her," I admitted. "But after Kyla saw you at the mall there's no way I was taking any chances. Especially since Anne would—I mean, she's my friend, but not the kind of friend who . . ." I struggled to figure out how to explain the Anne situation and then gave up. "It would be bad if she saw us. Really bad."

Rina looked at me. "Wait a minute. So your big plan

was to tell me to *run away*? I totally thought there was a guy with a gun and we were about to get shot or something."

"Yeah," I said, laughing in spite of myself. "I sort of realized halfway through that it wasn't a good idea, but you'd already taken off, so . . ."

"And then I couldn't remember where the car was, so I ended up running in a circle and all these people were staring at me like they thought I was crazy!" Rina started laughing too.

"Believe me, the same thing was happening on my end," I said. "I tripped on my shoelace at one point. It wasn't cute." I pressed my foot on the gas. Our narrow escape (or possibly just idiotic sprint through the parking lot) was several minutes behind us, and I was beginning to calm down. Of course, since the panic had subsided, my general feeling of needing to constantly study was back. Especially since I had no idea how much work I'd end up having to do on the robot this weekend. Jake had promised to take a crack at the calculations and then drop them off for me to review, but for all I knew he'd give me drawings of tap-dancing giraffes. When I'd asked him when I could expect his contribution he'd shrugged and said, "Sometime," which wasn't exactly conducive to my idea of time management—or anyone's, for that matter.

"Um . . . wanna quiz me on some more French?" I asked.

"Sure," said Rina, getting out the flash cards again. She picked one up and turned to me. "You know," she said thoughtfully, "maybe that wasn't Anne. Maybe that was just Anne's mysterious twin that came out of the computer."

"Oh, you bitch," I smirked.

"Just sayin'," she answered, grinning. She shuffled my deck of flash cards.

So this was life with a sister?

It wasn't too bad.

SATURDAY, DECEMBER 8

- Essay! I MEAN IT THIS TIME!
- Yearbook meeting
- E-mail Carmen re help w/ volleyball flyers
- E-mail prom committee re DJ vs. band (google local DJs? Student DJ?)
- Finals—amendment list for govt, French vocab & essay Q's, bio diagrams
- SAT practice at least 4 sections
- Robot calculations (possibly do this Sunday if really rocking out on SAT crap)
- Essay critiques for Renner
- Work out? Probably not ☹

SUNDAY, DECEMBER 9

- ESSAY! UNLESS YOU GOT IT DONE YESTERDAY, IN WHICH CASE YOU ARE A ROCK STAR!
- School board meeting
- Dinner/study break with Paul
- ~~Study break with girls? Did I say yes to this?~~ NO
- English paper
- All the stuff on Saturday you were supposed to do but probably didn't
- AAAAAAAAAAAARRRRRRGGGGGGGGGGGHHHHHHHHHHHHHHHHHHH

(Quit being so melodramatic)

CHAPTER ELEVEN
SATURDAY, DECEMBER 8

MY MOM WAS STANDING IN OUR KITCHEN, peering into the freezer. "Kate?" she asked. "What happened to all the frozen pizzas?" She was dressed in her usual "it's Saturday but I'm still going to the office" outfit of black pants and an untucked button-down, and her face was puzzled.

I looked up from the kitchen table, where I was nursing a cup of coffee and staring into my biology textbook. I knew exactly what she was talking about: two days ago there had been six Stouffer's frozen French bread pizzas in the freezer, and now there was only one.

"Yeah, sorry, I've been stress-eating," I said. That wasn't exactly a lie—I definitely had been. But my stress-eating was confined mostly to candy bars out of the school vending machines, whereas the pizzas were all Rina.

"Oh, to be seventeen and have that metabolism again," my mom said.

"Yep, that's me," I said. "Burning calories like a jack-rabbit." I got out of my chair and hopped up and down to illustrate my point, then walked over to the sink to rinse my coffee mug. My mom smiled and wrote "frozen pizza" on the grocery list stuck to the fridge, then picked up her purse and car keys from the kitchen table. She swung her coat over her shoulder and called, "Might be home late!" as she walked out the door.

I closed my bio book and smiled to myself. Rina and I had gotten used to sharing my room, and she'd made a cozy little space for herself in the walk-in closet with my sleeping bag and a flashlight for reading. But with my mom gone all day, we both had the run of the house.

"Be back in an hour or so!" I yelled up the stairs. I couldn't fathom why our yearbook advisor, Mr. Butler, had picked the weekend before finals to discuss sales strategies for the ad pages, but four student editors couldn't exactly stage an uprising against a teacher.

"Okay!" Rina's voice came floating down from the upstairs hallway, followed by the sound of running feet. She appeared at the bottom of the staircase just as I was on my way out. "Here," she said. "I noticed you like flash cards, so I made you some for government." She handed me a stack of index cards.

"Oh! Oh my God," I said, flipping through the cards. They were numbered one through twenty-seven on one side and had neatly printed descriptions of the constitutional amendments on the other. "Wow, these are great. Thanks." I put the cards into my bag.

"You're welcome!" said Rina. "You've got so much to do. I figured it would help you out a little. By the way, do you think after your Yale visit is over, we could talk about me going to journalism school?"

"Um . . . what?" I raised an eyebrow.

"Well, I can't just sit around our room the rest of my life, can I?" Rina asked cheerfully. "Maybe not journalism, maybe poli-sci or prelaw—I'm not sure yet." She waved at me and went into the living room, and I heard the muffled noise of the TV clicking on as I went into the garage. I mean, I *had* planned on figuring out what to do with Rina once hell week was over, but I was aiming more along the lines of sending her back into the computer game, not getting her into college. I had my own getting-into-college problems.

The yearbook meeting, however, was no longer one of them. "Canceled," said my coeditor Liza, who burst out of the school door to the parking lot just as I was reaching out my hand to open it. "Butler moved it to next week, time TBD. He's gonna e-mail us."

My eyes widened and I turned around and followed Liza, who had whooshed by me and was now briskly walking toward her car. "He moved it to *finals week*?" I asked.

"Oh my God, I'm so screwed!" The last thing I needed was an eleventh-hour change to my study schedule.

Liza looked back at me quizzically. "What're you talking about? This is awesome. Now we don't have to be in school on a Saturday!" She got in her car and took off, yelling, "Canceled!" out the window at an arriving car, which promptly turned around and left. Suddenly I was alone, staring at a bunch of empty parking spaces as the wind whipped my hair around my face.

Well, nothing to do but go home. *It'll be fine*, I told myself as I unlocked my driver's side door. The reschedule would clearly put a dent in next week, but at least it meant I had an extra hour right now, which I could use to work on my essay. And I had to admit that it would be nice to go up to my room, kick off my shoes, and change back into sweats.

Except that as I turned the corner onto my street and drove toward my house, I noticed a strange car in the driveway.

This could not be good.

I parked a few houses away—if there was someone in there with Rina, the last thing I wanted to do was alert them to another me arriving on the premises. I then inched toward my house from an angle, in case anyone suddenly came out the front door, and sneaked around to the backyard. I edged up to the living room window and peeked in. The curtains were slightly open, a point against Rina, since she was supposed to close them, but at least I could see inside.

Someone *was* in there with Rina.

It was Jake.

What the—?

I instinctively ducked down, crouching in the dead grass and wincing as my knees bonked against the outside wall of the house. Then I peeked my head up over the windowsill again. They were sitting on the living room couch; Jake in ratty jeans and an even rattier T-shirt, Rina in yoga pants and one of my tank tops. His feet were resting on the coffee table; hers were curled under her. The TV was on, but they weren't watching it; they were talking. And from the smiles on their faces, they were both having a dandy time.

Weird.

I kept watching, feeling like a creepy voyeur, but not even considering looking away. Jake was leaning toward Rina, apparently really interested in what she was saying, and Rina was smiling and twisting locks of her hair around her fingers. What could they possibly be talking about? Physics? It had to be physics, right?

Suddenly Rina laughed and shoved Jake a little. Then, instead of backing away to her original position, she stayed close.

Oh my God. Was she flirting?

I blinked in disbelief, then looked at them again. Rina was relaxing so far into the cushions of the couch that her head was practically on his shoulder. Christ, she *was* flirting!

I looked down at my phone, then at my car keys, trying to figure out the best way to stop this as quickly as possible. Should I call the home number? No, I'd told Rina to let the answering machine get everything. Should I go back to my car and pull into the garage, knowing that Rina would hear it and retreat to the closet? Yes, that was probably the best plan. I grabbed my bag and started to get up from my crouching position, and as I glanced through the window I saw Jake and Rina again.

Except this time they were kissing.

Aaaaaaaaaggggggggghhhhhhhhhhh!!!!!!!!!!!!!!!!!!!

I actually yelped in horror, then sprinted back around to the front of the house. What? How? A million thoughts flew through my mind, but first I had to stop the atrocity in my living room. *Immediately.* I looked at Jake's car and wondered if it had an alarm, then eyed the big decorative rocks around one of the trees in the front yard and wondered if I had the balls to throw one through his car window. No. I didn't. Instead, I rang the doorbell ten times in a row, which made absolutely no sense but at least would distract them; then I hid at the side of the house. A few moments later, Jake got in his car and drove away. As soon as he was out of sight, I sprinted in the front door and found Rina still in the living room.

"WHAT DID YOU JUST DO?!?" I screamed at her. "WHAT THE HELL DID YOU JUST DO?"

She looked taken aback. "Oh my God, calm down," she said, stepping away from me as if she was afraid I was going to hit her. Smart girl.

"I will *not* calm down!" I screamed, pacing around the room and looking for something to throw. I settled for punching a couch cushion. "Do you realize what you just did?"

"Yeah, I just kissed a boy for the first time!" Rina squealed. "And it was *awesome!*"

"You can't kiss that one!" I yelled. I picked up the cushion I'd just punched and gripped it tightly in my hands to keep from punching something else—namely, Rina's face.

"Why not?" she asked. She looked confused. "He's not Paul. You just said to stay away from Paul."

"Yeah, but—"

"So what's the problem?" she asked, sitting down in the armchair next to the couch. "Jake's cute! And really easy to talk to! He came by to drop off your physics stuff, and—"

"He thinks you're me!" I yelled, spiking the couch cushion onto the floor and then kicking it. I was this close to slamming her head into the coffee table.

"That's great!" Rina said. "That means he likes *you!*"

"No," I said, my voice icy with anger, "That means he thinks I'm a girl who cheats on her boyfriend! And it also means that he thinks *I* like *him*! Do you not get it? What the hell part of this don't you get?"

Rina stared at me, wide-eyed. "Oh," she said finally. "Right. I'm sorry."

"Not as sorry as I'm gonna be if—oh my God, what if he tells someone? Paul's gonna break up with me!" I felt a moment of sheer, blind panic, and I frantically looked around the room as if help were magically going to arrive from somewhere, bursting out of the walls or materializing in the fireplace. "If anybody hears about this, they're totally gonna tell, and it's gonna get back to Paul somehow, and then he's gonna—"

"Nobody's gonna hear about it," said Rina. "Don't worry."

"How the hell do you know? Jake could be telling half the world by now!" Oh my God, I had to text Paul. No, I had to call Paul. But what was I going to say? I opened my phone, saw the picture of Paul that I have as a background, freaked out, and closed it again and threw it onto the couch. No. *No panic-texting*, I told myself. *That's even worse than drunk-texting*. Calm down. I just had to calm down.

"Jake won't say anything," Rina said. "He just doesn't seem like that kind of person, you know? You *should* know. Didn't you used to be friends?"

"You guys talked about that?"

"Sure," Rina shrugged. "We talked about a bunch of stuff. Did you know he wants to go to art school?"

"Yeah, I think so," I said distractedly. "He likes drawing."

"Painting too. He said he might want to be a storyboard artist for movies or something. Oh, and he drew this little cartoon of me. Or you." She dug a Post-it note out of the couch cushions and held it out, a little ink drawing of a wavy-haired girl wearing a minidress and a cape, done vaguely anime style. It was super cute.

Christ.

I sank down onto the end of the couch that was farther away from Rina, hugged a throw pillow to my chest (both for comfort and to have it ready to chuck at her head if necessary), and closed my eyes.

"Kate?" asked Rina in a small voice.

"Yeah," I answered flatly, keeping my eyes closed.

"I'm sorry."

"You said that already."

"I know, but I really am," Rina said. "I wasn't thinking. I mean, it's just—he was flirting with me, and—"

I opened my eyes and sat up. "*He* was flirting with *you*? Because from what I saw, *you* were the one getting all up in his face." I pasted on a goofy grin and twirled my hair in my fingers, imitating what I'd seen her doing.

"Yeah, but he was all, you know, smiley and nice, so I figured—"

"Smiley and nice? Jake is never smiley and nice," I snapped. "He's occasionally not a jerk, but it's usually, like, grudgingly. Begrudgingly. Whatever." Through my still-simmering rage, I mentally cursed Jake for not texting me before dropping off the robot specs. How rude was he, just swinging by my house like that? Or maybe it was my own fault. I should've made him set a specific time instead of agreeing to play it by ear. Then none of this would have happened.

Wait, why was I blaming myself? This was all on Rina. "Why the *hell* did you open the door?" I yelled.

"Maybe you should try being nicer to him," Rina said, ignoring my question. "It was pretty mean of you to ditch him just because Paul thought he was a slacker."

"That is *not* how it happened."

Rina shrugged. "According to him it was. So I was like, yeah, sorry about that. And then he kind of warmed up and got friendlier. . . ."

"Yeah," I snapped. "I saw." I felt absolutely sick. The things Rina had said to Jake, Jake now thought *I* had said. And there wasn't anything I could do about it. There was also nothing I could do about the image of them kissing—which was pretty much a visual of *me* and Jake kissing—that was now permanently burned into my eyeballs.

Rina suddenly got up. "I know what'll make you feel better!" she said, running upstairs.

"You never coming back down because you've somehow disappeared?" I called after her.

"Don't be mean!" came her muffled reply. In a minute she returned with some papers in her hand. "Here," she said, giving me the thin, neatly stapled stack. "I was saving it for tomorrow, but—"

"What is this?" I asked. I looked at it. It looked like an English paper on *The Sound and the Fury*. I scanned through the pages. It *was* an English paper on *The Sound and the Fury*. It was due Monday, actually, for my take-home final, except I hadn't written it yet.

"I wrote it for you!" Rina said cheerfully. "I saw in your planner that it was due Monday, and you've been so stressed, so yesterday I looked at your notes from class, and the stuff you highlighted in the book, and then I wrote it for you!"

"What? Why the hell would you do that?"

"You're stressed," she repeated. "I thought it would help you out. You know, like the flash cards."

I flung the paper aside. "No! I mean, I can't. Flash cards are one thing, but a whole paper is just . . . sketchy."

"Then let me help you some other way," Rina insisted. "Please? I know I screwed up, so if there's anything I can do, seriously, anything—"

"No," I said.

"Anything!" Rina declared again. She plunked down on the couch so that she was at my eye level and looked at me pleadingly.

I stared at her, completely unable to believe her nerve. She had just spent the morning deliberately impersonating me, quite possibly wrecking my relationship with my boyfriend and probably every single other aspect of my social life as well, and she thought writing a paper would make up for it?

"It doesn't have to be homework," Rina said. "I could . . . I don't know, do your laundry for you, if that would save you some time, or I could clean your room, or—"

"Yes," I said suddenly, sitting up. "Yes, there is something you can do." I felt simultaneously sick to my stomach and delighted at the thought that had just occurred to me.

"What is it?" Rina asked eagerly. "Anything. I swear."

I spit my words out quickly before I started thinking too hard about the possible consequences. "You can go to the school board meeting tomorrow afternoon," I told her. "I'm the student rep for Colchester, but all I do is sit there. I don't even take notes." I took a deep breath. "So . . . what if *you* went and sat there instead? And then I'll have an extra hour to write my English paper. My *own* English paper," I added.

Rina's eyes widened. "Oh my God. Yes!" she whooped. "Of course! I will totally do that. It'll be so fun!"

I glared at her.

"Or . . . not fun?" she asked, in a slightly quieter voice.

"Not fun," I answered. "Zero fun. You go, sit down, shut up, and come straight back. Okay? That's all. No talking to anyone. No going anywhere else. "

"Okay," she said, nodding. An excited smile crept across her face again, and I intensified my glare.

"Don't you dare have a good time," I snapped. "It's the least you can do after today. The absolute *least*."

"I know," she said, her smile abruptly disappearing. "And I'm sorry, again."

Silence.

"Is there anything else I can do?" she finally asked, after a long, tense beat of both of us just sitting on the couch.

"Yeah," I said. "Go in the closet and don't come out for the rest of the day."

Rina nodded, got up, and slowly went up the stairs.

Dear Diary,

Guess where I am right now. AT A SCHOOL BOARD
MEETING! This is *so cool* that I get to be out of the house! And
you know what's even cooler? Kate let me take her car! Okay, so
she made me practice up and down the street first because she
didn't believe me when I said I could drive (and she was right,
actually—I'd never done it before). But guess what, turns out I'm
an *awesome* driver! Who knew how much you could learn from
reading and watching TV?

And this meeting is so exciting!

Okay, actually it's boring, but I mean, you know, the idea of it
is exciting. Getting to be out of the house and stuff.

Okay, actually, no. Now it's just really boring.

Kate's really gotta find a better way to spend her time.

Love, Rina

CHAPTER TWELVE
SUNDAY, DECEMBER 9

TICK. TICK. SCCCRITCH-TICK. TICK. **I WAS SITTING** at the kitchen table late Sunday afternoon, listening to the messed-up second hand on the clock above the pantry door and typing my English paper on my laptop. Thanks to Rina taking the school board meeting off my hands, I felt calmer about schoolwork than I had in a while. But it was also a little hard to concentrate, given that I kept flashing back to Rina and Jake's kiss. I'd talked to Kyla on the phone, but luckily she hadn't heard any interesting gossip. Later I'd talked to Paul as well, and all seemed normal with him. Still, one word from Jake to the wrong person, and the story would be around school like wildfire.

"Hello?" called Rina's voice from the front hall. She burst into the kitchen, threw off her coat, and sank into the chair across from me. "Those meetings suck," she declared. "I mean, thanks for letting me go, but why do you even bother?"

"I'll make a note of that for next time," I said. She had a point, but I wasn't really one to skip things I was supposed to be at. If I were, I would've started peacing out on school board meetings eons ago, not to mention National Honor Society and half my other extracurriculars. "Did anybody talk to you?"

Rina shook her head. "Cool," I said, relieved. "Well, I'm either gonna work on my essay or do some SAT stuff until Paul gets here. . . ." I trailed off as I tried to decide which.

Rina perked up. "He's coming over?"

I gave her a warning glance. "Yes. For a study break." I sighed. "Although I'll probably still be studying, even while he's here."

"Then why invite him?"

"Well, we haven't seen each other much lately and he's starting to complain—"

"That's so cute!" Rina exclaimed. "He misses you!"

"I know, I know," I said, "and he's totally right. But he sort of doesn't get that this is, like, the busiest week of my whole life. He never has to study as much as I do, and right now I have to more than ever, so . . ." Rina nodded sympathetically and I realized I was rambling. Not that she minded. Or noticed. "Anyway," I said. "I'm gonna go upstairs. Mom's at the office till late, so do whatever." I got up from the table.

"Cool, I'll watch TV," Rina said. "And I'll make you some Euro flash cards."

Sweet.

Half an hour later, I'd gotten zero wrong on an SAT math section. "Yay!" I said, then slammed the practice book shut, blowing some papers off my desk. I bent to pick them up. It was mostly scrap paper, plus some AP history handouts from last year and a Post-it from Paul that just said "hi" with a smiley face (note to self: clean desk more often). The last thing I picked up was the English take-home Rina had written for me. I was about to chuck it in the trash, but out of curiosity, I flipped past the cover page and started reading.

It was good.

In fact, it was better than the one I had outlined in detail and was planning on finishing tonight. If I were grading it, I would've given myself (well, Rina) an A already, and I was barely on page two.

"Oh, are you gonna use that? You should totally use that," Rina said, suddenly poking her head in my bedroom door.

"Aaagh! Don't sneak up like that!" I said, almost dropping the paper.

"Sorry." Rina stepped into my room. "But are you gonna use that paper? Because technically . . ." She paused and smiled, her voice taking on a hint of deviousness. "It's not like it's actually cheating. You and I are the same person, and if I wrote it, that means you wrote it. Plus, I used all of your notes. See?"

"That logic is sketchy at best and totally evil at worst," I said.

"Just sayin'." She shrugged, the look on her face somehow blending innocence and "I dare you."

"Tempting . . . very tempting," I said, "but nope. I can't do it." I crumpled up the paper into a ball.

"The file's still on your computer," Rina singsonged.

"Only until I delete it," I replied, parroting her tone of voice. I threw the wad of crumpled-up paper at her, and she giggled and went back downstairs.

A little later Paul rang the doorbell, and Rina dashed up the stairs to hide. "Hi!" I said, opening the door and stepping back so he could come in. He was wearing his letter jacket over a Celtics hoodie and carrying two large pizza boxes. He raised the pizzas in the air as I hugged him around the waist and dragged him down to the basement. I threw on the lights and we skittered over the cold cement floor near the stairs toward the carpeted section in front of the TV.

"Hello, stranger," Paul said, putting the pizza boxes on the carpet and sitting down next to them. He smiled at me and leaned back against the couch, stretching out his long legs.

"Shut it," I said. "It's not my fault!" I sat down next to Paul, carefully studying his face for any signs that he'd heard something about Jake since the last time I'd talked to him. Thankfully, there was nothing but his now-standard expression of slight exasperation at my overly busy schedule.

"Fair enough," he said, putting a slice of veggie pizza onto a paper plate and handing it to me. "Some of it's mine, and I apologize once again for bailing on Friday. How was the shopping? Did you get me anything?"

"Perhaps," I said, looking around innocently. "Perhaps a supplement to a previously purchased gift or gifts."

He grinned. "Awesome. But actually, what I really, really want for Christmas—"

"Do not say 'threesome.'"

"—is more time with my girlfriend."

"Awww, how sweet!" I said, before I realized the implications of the words *threesome* and *girlfriend* as they related to Rina being in my room that very second, and almost burst out laughing. My subsequent facial contortions drew a weird look from Paul.

"Sorry," I said, shaking my head and trying to will the giggles away. "I'm just, um, stressed out. By the way, do you care if I study while we eat?" I pulled some flash cards out of my back pocket.

Paul's hand, which had been on its way to his mouth with a slice of pizza, stopped in midair. "Seriously?" he asked, rolling his eyes.

"I just want to take advantage of every minute."

Paul sighed. "What's up with you lately? You used to manage your time so much better."

"Oh, gee," I answered, bristling at his insultingly frustrated tone of voice, "I'm so *sorry* that I'm trying to get into Yale with you."

"Yeah, I know, but I didn't think it would turn you into some sort of neurotic, study-all-the-time—"

"I mean maybe you didn't realize this, but I can't magically get straight A's just by being alive, unlike some people—"

"Of course you can—you've been doing it for years."

"No," I said flatly. "I haven't."

Paul looked confused. "Huh?"

"I said, I haven't been—"

The doorbell interrupted my oncoming rant. Paul raised an "are you expecting someone?" eyebrow. I shrugged, glad that what was about to turn into an argument had been headed off at the pass, and stood up. I went to the front door and looked out the window. Kyla and Anne were on my porch, and I could see Carmen's car idling on the curb, with our other friends Tess and Laurin inside.

"Oh. Hey guys," I said, as I opened the door. "What's going—"

"Mandatory study break!" declared Kyla. She was wearing a corduroy mini and a puffy down vest over a black shirt that seemed to be made mostly of lace. I had no idea how she wasn't freezing to death.

"What?" I asked.

"You heard the woman," Anne said. Her blond hair was pulled back tightly as usual, and the tops of her ears were already reddening in the cold. "You fully said okay before, remember I texted you?" Oh. Ohhhh. Right. I dimly remembered scheduling hang time with the girls in my planner. I also remembered telling myself that I would cancel, but apparently I'd forgotten that part.

"All right then," said Kyla, promptly interpreting the realization on my face in her favor. "You remember. So get your ass in the car or the car will back over your ass."

Paul appeared behind me. "Ladies," he said, pulling on his jacket and getting his car keys out of his pocket.

"Man," intoned Kyla, deepening her voice to match (or at least get closer to) his. Anne giggled, then her eyes flicked from Paul to me and back to Paul again. I got a weird feeling that she could feel the whisper of tension between us, so I was relieved when Paul pulled me into the kitchen, out of sight of the front door.

"I thought you were supposed to ditch your friends before me," he said, his voice barely audible.

"I know, and I meant to, but I forgot to tell them," I whispered back as quickly as I could. "I didn't realize they were actually going to show up. I'm sorry. Like you said, I'm totally disorganized lately. . . ."

Paul sighed. "Well, whatever. You might as well go. But

call me later." He kissed me, then edged his way past the girls on the porch and jogged out to his car. Anne and I both watched him leave.

"Okay, so, boyfriend time over, friend time begins," said Kyla. She looked at me impatiently, and I could see that she wasn't about to let me bail. But my English paper was waiting, as was my personal statement, and I knew that a half-hour coffee break would turn into an hour, and then into three. There was no way in hell I could go.

Then it hit me: Rina could.

Oh my God. I'd been killing myself to get everything done and keep everyone happy and I had this identical twin doing absolutely nothing upstairs.

Rina could go in my place!

"I'll be down in five minutes," I told Kyla.

"You'd better be!" she said cheerfully. "We've almost forgotten what you look like. Which, by the way, is terrible. Maybe *more* makeup during these stressful study times, not less." She grinned and walked back toward her car. Anne followed her, and I shut the door, sprinted upstairs and found Rina in the closet.

"Feel like going out with my friends?"

"What?" she practically shrieked.

"Shhh," I said. "They're all outside. Paul just left, but I forgot to tell them I didn't have time to hang this weekend. You wanna go grab coffee with them? Pretend to be me?"

"Oh my God, yes!" Rina said.

"Okay, quick, switch clothes," I said, and we both threw off our shirts and pants so we could trade. My hair was up, so I grabbed Rina a ponytail holder, and while we were changing outfits I tried to give her a nutshell rundown of my friends. "You've seen all these girls in the pictures, so you should be fine, but really quickly: Kyla's the redhead. Laurin's the tallest. Tess has dark brown hair; she's the really buff one. Anne's the sort of uptight blond. Carmen's wearing her glasses today, so—"

"Doesn't she always wear them?" asked Rina. She put her hair in a ponytail.

"What?" I asked.

"Carmen," said Rina. "You just said she's wearing her glasses today like it's a weird thing, but in the pictures, she's always wearing them."

"Oh," I said. "Right. Yes." I generally think of Carmen as a no-glasses person because she always puts her contacts in for volleyball, but Rina was actually right. Since the season ended, she'd been rocking the librarian frames every day.

"Okay, well, anyway," I said, as Rina plucked my watch off my wrist and put it on her own, then fixed her hair once more, "that should cover you. If there's something you don't know, just act spacey and plead exhaustion, because frankly that's how I feel now anyway." I was slightly worried that

Rina wouldn't be able to pull off a convincing impression of me in front of so many people at once, but I also realized the advantage of sending her out in the field, so to speak, to listen for any inklings that the Jake story had gotten around. And if they did notice something was off with me, it wasn't like they'd guess that I'd sent my SimuLife twin out in my place.

"Okay!" she said, just as Kyla, in the driveway, started leaning on her car horn. "How do I look?" She was now in the navy blue waffle-weave shirt and jeans I'd just been wearing, and I was in her workout pants and a long-sleeved gray thermal.

"Just like me," I said, smiling. "Thanks for this! Have fun, and if my mom is home by the time you guys get back, I'll sit by the living room window and you can tap on it and we'll figure out a way to sneak you in."

"Got it!" Rina waved and sprinted down the stairs, grabbing one of my coats and shrugging into it on her way out the door. I peeked out the window as she ran outside and got into Kyla's car. The little white Jetta pulled out into the dark, followed by Carmen's Prius, and I suddenly realized that I should've given Rina some money. I turned to the dresser, and saw that my bag was tipped over, my half-empty wallet spilling out of it. Oh. I guess Rina had thought of everything.

I breathed a sigh of relief and turned to my computer,

where my *Sound and the Fury* take-home final was waiting on the screen. For the first time in forever, I felt like I could handle everything. I didn't have to worry about letting my friends down. I didn't even have to worry as much about studying for finals, thanks to the piles of flash cards and color-coded outlines Rina had left on my desk. Sure, she'd created some problems—the Jake thing still made my stomach twist nervously. But she was also saving my ass.

I turned to my English paper, poised my fingers over the keyboard, and started typing.

Dear Diary,

Hanging out with Kate's friends was sooooo much fun! I
have to figure out a way to do this more often. *Have.* To. There
was one scary moment when Anne asked if she'd seen me (well,
Kate) at the outlets on Friday, and I had to be like, "Whaaaaat? Oh,
no, totally not, that wasn't me," and then Kyla was all like, "Wow,
that's been happening to you a lot lately." She wasn't really suspicious or anything though. Anne seemed to be, but I did a good job
covering.

Of course, when I got home and told Kate about it, she
totally freaked out. Like, *totally*. She's really scared of getting
caught, and she started going off on Anne. But I think she's just
panicking because she's really stressed out (like, *really*—she's
trying to hide it, but I can totally tell). Besides, it only took about
three seconds with the girls before the subject of mysterious look-
alikes turned into something about twins in general, and then into
something about the Olsen twins, and then into whether Laurin
would rather bone Robert Pattinson in Cedric Diggory mode or
Twilight mode. She was leaning toward *Twilight* mode, but then
scrapped it and went with Kevin Garnett. I don't know who that is.

Love, Rina

CHAPTER THIRTEEN
MONDAY, DECEMBER 10

MY ALARM CLOCK ONLY MANAGED TO RING half a *fwamp* on Monday morning before I reached out my hand to slap it off, so hard that it fell from the nightstand to the floor with a dull thump. Then I just lay in bed, covers up to my chin, eyes wide, staring at the ceiling. Outside my window, the sun was nowhere near coming up yet, and I could practically feel the cold from the frost-covered window reaching across the room toward me.

I so did not want to go to school today.

I inched a toe out from under the covers and let it adjust to the cooler, nonblanketed air. While the rest of the school might not know about Rina's illicit (and awful, and horrifying, and disgusting, and horrifying, and awful, and hey, that was sort of a palindrome) kiss, Jake still knew. And I had no choice but to see him later today.

Yikes.

In English I handed in my not-as-good-as-Rina's take-home exam; then, thanks to Ms. Appenfore letting the class use the hour as a study hall, I tried to start my essay. Unfortunately, the only subjects that occurred to me in thirty minutes of staring at the screen were, "What's Up with Jake?" "I Wonder How I Should Act When I See Jake?" "My Lab Partner's Current Thoughts and Emotions," and "The Mind of the Buzz-Cut Asian Dude." I finally gave up and forced myself to finish going over the essays Ms. Renner had given me. At the very least, concentrating on correcting someone else's grammar meant less time spent visualizing embarrassing Jake-centric scenarios. I ended up getting jealous that the other kids were writing about cool, random stuff like designing and sewing their own clothes, or their pet Angora rabbit scaring the hell out of people who didn't know what it was. I was particularly impressed-slash-annoyed by the one titled "Thirty Parties in Thirty Days," which, though glaringly inappropriate for a college essay, was incredibly fun to read. I was pretty sure I hadn't been to thirty parties in my entire high school career.

And then suddenly it was last period and I was sitting at my lab table in physics. "Uh, hey," I said over the sound of the bell as Jake sat down next to me. He was wearing tan cords and a black T-shirt with a skull and crossbones on the front, and I inwardly winced at the shirt's appropriateness.

"Hey," he replied, grinning. Uh-oh. That already wasn't good. But his smile faded when he saw the look on my face, and disappeared completely when I muttered, "I kind of need to talk to you about Saturday but I don't wanna do it in class. So can we just get this over with and I'll talk to you after?" I opened up my physics binder in as businesslike a manner as possible.

"Yeah," he answered, his face neutral, all traces of his good mood gone. He scooted his chair marginally farther away from me, and neither of us said anything the rest of the hour except for the bare necessities, like, "Can you hand me that?" and, "I think you've got the angle of that trajectory wrong." When the bell rang, he followed me out of the classroom and into a side hall. The hall emptied quickly as everyone headed out the doors toward home.

"Um, so . . . Saturday." I set my book bag on the floor and leaned back against the wall, nervously pulling my shirt sleeves down over my hands.

"Yeah." Jake was standing stiffly a few feet away, his face unreadable. He crossed his arms, then uncrossed them, then crossed them again, the fingers of his right hand fiddling with the edge of his left T-shirt sleeve.

"That wasn't—did you tell anyone about that?" I asked.

"Of course not."

"Thank *God*," I blurted. Jake glared at me. I flushed

with embarrassment, realizing how insulting my obvious relief must sound.

"Sorry, that didn't come out right," I said, my words starting to speed up. "But I mean—look, I'm sorry, but that just wasn't really me that day, if that makes any sense. I wasn't thinking straight, and again, I'm really sorry, and it's probably best if we could just forget it ever happened." I took a deep breath. "Okay?"

"Sure, fine," Jake answered simply. He suddenly seemed kind of checked out. He shoved his hands into his pockets and stared at the graffiti along the edge of a bulletin board a few feet away, which read, "If you can read this, good for you for being literate, and if you are still reading this, you are wasting a bunch of your own time, dumbass."

"Because I have a boyfriend and I don't want anyone to get the wrong idea," I added.

"Yeah, I know." Jake shifted on his feet like he was about to turn and walk away, not as an escape, but just totally casually. He didn't look mad or embarrassed. He didn't look sad; he didn't look happy—he didn't look anything. We might as well have been talking about the weather. Actually, if we'd been talking about the weather he might've been more engaged, since he'd been complaining last week that it sort of creeped him out when it was both sunny and cold at the same time, and today was one of those days.

"So . . . I guess that's it," I said uncertainly. A million

questions flew through my mind. Was he mad at me? Did he think it was all just a lark? Did kissing "me" mean anything to him? Did he actually *like* me? But this conversation clearly wasn't headed in that direction.

"Cool." Jake started to walk off.

"I just didn't want it to be awkward or anything. . . ."

Jake turned around and came back. "So don't make it awkward," he said, a hint of a smile forming at the corners of his mouth.

"I'm trying not to," I said.

"By dragging me out in the hallway and rambling at me?" Jake's eyes betrayed amusement and his voice had regained its usual snark.

"Oh, shut up," I said, picking up my book bag and swinging it so that it lightly bonked him on the arm.

"I mean, I'd love to sit here and listen to you go on and on about how you want to pretend something never happened," Jake continued, "because going on and on about something is totally the best way to pretend it never happened." He smirked at me.

"Okay, you made your point," I said, smiling back at him. "End of story."

"Cool, see ya tomorrow then." He ambled away down the hall.

"Bye," I called to his retreating back. He waved over his shoulder without looking.

Well.

I shook my head a little as I slung my bag over my shoulder and started walking toward my car. I was glad the whole kiss fiasco had been so easy to clear up, but a tiny part of me was also annoyed. Apparently, I'd spent most of my weekend worrying over something that had turned out to be not a big deal at all. Not even a medium deal. Or a small deal. In fact, it was a total lack of deal, and while it was certainly better than if he'd flipped out and gotten angry, it also meant that the time and energy I'd spent on thinking about this had been completely and totally wasted. Plus, much as I hated to admit it, there was a part of me that was a little—not disappointed, really, but—surprised, I guess, that Jake really didn't seem to care. Either that, or he had an Oscar-winning acting career in his future.

But it was an extreme relief to know that I didn't have to worry about losing my boyfriend. *Hell, maybe I can even get an essay topic out of this*, I thought to myself as I unlocked my car door and got in. "It's Totally Okay to Guilt Your Twin into Doing Menial Tasks for You Even Though Her Ill-Advised Make-Out Session Did Nobody Any Harm"?

Clearly my brain was beginning to break down.

Rina's face peeked out from an upstairs window as I drove up to my house. She met me at the door, practically bouncing on her tiptoes, and dragged me upstairs to show me that she'd washed, folded, and shelved my laundry, and then dusted every surface in my room.

"I didn't move anything, don't worry. I know you've got your whole system right now for finals and stuff," she said, indicating the piles of books and papers she'd left on the floor exactly where they were supposed to be, and then eagerly running her hand over the top of my computer monitor and bookshelves to demonstrate how completely dust-free they were.

"Wow," I said, looking around. "Thanks."

"Still trying to make up for that Jake thing," she said. "Least I could do."

"Well, I talked to him," I told her. "He didn't tell anyone, thank God. And he seems to have already sort of forgotten about it, or is at least pretending to, which is good enough for me."

"Oh." She looked a little crestfallen before perking back up. "That's awesome! Now you don't have to worry— it's like it never happened!" She clapped her hands.

"Hey," I said, a note of warning in my voice, "just because this one thing turned out okay doesn't mean it always will, so don't go getting too enthusiastic. Next thing you know, you'll be hooking up with half the football team and everyone at school will be calling me Kate Fellate."

Rina giggled. "Ha! That's hilarious!"

"Oh, shut up. You know what I mean." I glared at her.

"Yeah, I do," she said. "Sorry. So how was school?"

"Fine." I disentangled myself from my coat and inched toward my computer.

"How're the girls?" Rina bounced onto my bed and looked at me expectantly. "Did they say anything about last night?"

"Not really," I answered, opening up my government notes and pulling up the pages on the last several Supreme Courts. "I think Kyla might've mocked me for being spaced out, but that's not exactly a weird occurrence."

"Did Laurin say anything about Steve Suarez?" Rina asked.

I turned to her, surprised. "Something's up with Laurin and Steve Suarez?"

"Yeah," she said. "Didn't I tell you when I got back? Oh my God, I'm sorry!"

"No, it's fine, it's not like I asked." I hadn't. Rina had gotten home after my mom, so after she'd sneaked back upstairs, we'd only talked a little, in case my mom overheard. She had read (speedily flipping between Harry Potter book four, *Wuthering Heights*, and two issues of *Allure*), and I'd studied until we both fell asleep. I was bummed that I'd missed out on some crucial gossip. Laurin had hooked up with Steve's brother Robby last year, but he'd graduated, and now apparently she'd moved on to the younger model. Scandalous.

"So what happened with them?" I asked.

"Oh, nothing that I know of—that's why I was asking you," Rina said. "Laurin just said she was thinking about it."

"That little vixen," I said, grinning.

"Is she?" Rina asked.

"Not at all, actually. That's why this is somewhat big news."

"But Anne kind of is, huh?" Rina said. "That thing with Porter last year . . . And by the way, I think she has a crush on Paul."

I rolled my eyes. "Good observation skills," I told her. "That's been kicking around forever. And I can't really do anything about it because they're still friends."

"Eh, I wouldn't worry about her," Rina answered. "We're way hotter." She grinned at me. "So will you tell me everything you guys talked about today? At lunch or between classes or whatever? I want to make sure I don't miss out on anything."

"Uh . . . sure," I said, glancing back at my notes. "After I finish studying though, okay?"

"Okay!" We heard the garage door opening and Rina quickly retreated to the closet, grabbing the fifth Harry Potter book and one of my photo albums. "I can't wait to hear about everyone!" She sat down on her sleeping bag and nudged the door closed.

All of her questions felt a little weird, but clearly she

hadn't had much of a social life in SimuLife. And I was actually kind of looking forward to discussing all my friends with her and getting a second opinion on whether or not Kyla should dye her hair, or whether Carmen's twice-weekly pedicures were total overkill or just semi-overkill, or who Paul's friend Decker should date next. Hell, if Rina had shown up, say, late second semester after I'd already gotten into college and was cruising out the rest of the school year, things might've been very different.

But she hadn't. She'd shown up now. And I had work to do.

Bleh.

I turned back to my computer.

CHAPTER FOURTEEN
TUESDAY, DECEMBER 11

THE NEXT MORNING, I HIT THE SNOOZE button a split second after my alarm rang. "No," I half-mumbled, half-moaned, scrunching down and throwing the covers over my head.

Ten minutes later I did it again, falling back asleep so quickly that I didn't even register hitting the clock.

And then I did it again, reasoning that I could just eat a Clif bar in the car.

And then I did it again.

After that, either my alarm clock gave up and didn't bother ringing anymore, or I kept hitting snooze without even waking up. By the time I was poked awake by Rina's none-too-gentle finger in my ribs, I had nineteen minutes to make it into my desk in AP English.

Dammit.

"Morning!" Rina said. She was dressed in a pair of my

jeans and a red long-sleeved tee layered over a white one. Her hair looked cute—the dark brown waves were swept back from her face with a few bronze-colored bobby pins— and she was holding my book bag.

"Hi. Morning," I answered hastily. "I'm actually running reeeally late, so could you—" I flung my blanket aside and made a beeline for the shower, but Rina stood in the doorway and blocked my exit.

"Want me to go to school for you?" she asked. She held up my book bag, already packed for the day.

"Ha, hilarious," I said, elbowing her to the side. "Come on, I gotta hurry." All we were doing in English this week was giving oral presentations on the essays we'd turned in, but I needed to minimize my lateness in case I was called on today.

"Seriously," Rina said, following me down the hall. "I'm all ready, and you could go back to sleep if you want. You must be really tired to sleep in that long."

Hmmmm. That was true. I stopped walking.

"I read your English take-home exam," she continued, "so I could totally do your presentation. "

Tempting. I turned back and looked at Rina, who started talking faster.

"And then you can study all day. Like, *all* day. I also looked at your to-do list and started some things you didn't have time for." She held up a few sheets of computer printouts—apparently she had done some DJ research and drafted an e-mail for me to send to the prom committee, and then done the same thing for the yearbook superlative list. Wow.

"Well, can't say you're not convincing." I rubbed my eyes groggily. It vaguely occurred to me that if she'd been up early enough to get dressed and get ready for school, she should've woken me up on time. But she had some good points. It wasn't that big a deal if I didn't go to school today. English would be a waste of time, and every other class would probably be last-minute finals review. I'd be more efficient studying at home by myself. As for physics—well, I didn't have a problem with not having to face Jake. He'd seemed cool yesterday, but an afternoon of studying while Rina worked on the robot would be awesome. As long as she didn't make out with him in class or something—Jake, not the robot. Although I certainly hoped she didn't make out with the robot either.

"What the hell," I said, walking back into my bedroom and plunking down on the bed. "Sure. Go. But if you so much as look at Jake funny in physics—"

Rina broke into a huge grin and clapped her hands. "Cool!" she said. "And of course I won't do anything with Jake. You don't even have to say it, duh! Yay, thank you so much!" She slung my book bag over her shoulder, grabbed my coat, squeaked with excitement, and ran out the door.

I smiled for a moment, then looked down at my bed and scrunched the blankets in my hands. It was barely light outside, and under the covers it would be warm and cozy—I could totally go back to sleep. But the only reason I'd let Rina go to school was for the extra hours of study time, so . . .

Oh my God. I'd just let Rina go to school.

Where she'd be talking to everyone I knew. Including Paul.

What the hell was I thinking? Had I been sleepwalking?

I ran to the front window, but my car was already out of sight. Too late.

Well, no point obsessing, I told myself. I must have been more sleep-deprived than I thought to just let her walk out the door like that, but all I could do now was take advantage. I made my bed so it would be harder to collapse back into it, then sat down at my desk.

I studied for government.

I studied for Euro, making ample use of the flash cards Rina had made.

I watched a French movie that I'd DVRed a while back after Madame Bertrand had told us that it would seriously help on the listening comprehension section of our exam.

I took another shot at my Yale essay, although when I poised my fingers to type, the only thing that came out was a Google search for baby pandas. And then, all of a sudden,

I woke to the sound of Rina's footsteps pounding up the staircase.

"Hi!" she said breathlessly, bursting into my room and flinging herself onto my bed. "Oh, sorry, were you taking a nap?"

"Not on purpose," I said, sighing. Was the school day over already? I blinked my eyes a few times, then rubbed my forehead and realized that falling asleep face-first on my keyboard had imprinted squares all over it. I looked at my monitor and saw ten pages of n's printed across the entire screen.

At least my essay was no longer blank.

Dear Diary,

School is the most awesome thing ever! First of all, Kyla was totally surprised this morning when I got us both coffee (apparently Kate's been slacking off lately). Then I got called on in English to do the presentation, and I *kicked ass*! I made the whole class laugh, and I caught Paul looking at me all proudly, and I'm a hundred percent sure Ms. Appenfore gave me an A. I rocked all the other classes, too—took thorough notes and went through all of the review handouts and highlighted the most important parts for Kate. (She needs all the help she can get this week.) I offered to go back to school for her tomorrow, but she said no on account of finals. I tried to be like, "Exactly, and I could take them for you," but she still said no. Don't know why; I know I would do better on them than she would. No offense to her. She probably won't even wake up on time. Again, no offense to her.

But the more important thing is, I had so much fun today! Paul is really, really hot, and so funny and nice, and Jake was really nice, too, and even cuter than the day he came to our house. You know who else is cute? My French teacher's student teacher. It's not wrong—he's only, like, twenty-two. Okay, maybe it's a little wrong.

Love, Rina

CHAPTER FIFTEEN
WEDNESDAY, DECEMBER 12

"FEEL FREE TO THANK ME NOW," JAKE SAID, lazily leaning back in his chair. "Start any time." I was staring at the papers he had pushed across the lab table at me— his half of the project write-up, as well as a chart of all the test throws he wanted our robot to do.

"But I was going to make the chart," I said, unable to hide the shock in my voice as I flipped through the neatly typed pages. I stared at him, wondering if maybe Rina had done some sort of voodoo on him yesterday.

"No big deal, I just got to it first." Jake shrugged. "Don't look so shocked." He was wearing an ink-smudged white T-shirt, which smudged even further when he accidentally leaned forward onto his tabletop drawing of a dinosaur playing blackjack with a goat. After a moment of looking annoyed, he decided to roll with it, and started drawing on his shirt directly.

"Can't help it," I said. "Did you do a bunch of mood-altering drugs or something?"

"Perhaps," he answered.

"Can you keep doing them?"

"Perhaps," he said again. He shrugged, then grinned at me.

"Well, thank you," I said, grinning back and shoving him a little. "Thank you!" This day had suddenly gotten way better. I'd kicked ass on my French final (I was pretty sure) and done okay on Euro (I wasn't as sure, but it would have been waaay worse without Rina's flash cards), but Jake being both cool *and* hardworking was a welcome surprise.

"Hey." Anne appeared at our lab table and reached into our supply box. "So I can have these, right?" She held up a few lengths of gray rubber tubing.

"Sure," Jake answered, at the exact same moment I said, "Huh?"

"You said yesterday you weren't using these and we could have them," Anne repeated, nodding toward the far side of the room, where her lab partner was fiddling with their egg-drop contraption. "Remember?" She fixed her pale blue eyes on my face and gave me a studied, measured look.

"I did?" I asked, genuinely confused as Jake looked at me weirdly. *Rina.* Duh. "Right," I said quickly, blushing. "Sorry."

"No problem," Anne said lightly, looking a tiny bit triumphant. "I know you're really swamped this week. I'm sure it's not the first thing you forgot. Thanks." She turned around, blond hair swishing, and made her way back to her lab table as I cursed myself for not grilling Rina about every detail from yesterday. These were the mistakes that we couldn't afford, especially not with Anne paying so much attention. She was back at her own table, but, like she'd been doing the entire past week, she kept glancing over at Jake and me.

"You okay?" Jake asked.

I realized that one of my hands was gripping the edge of our lab table tightly enough to whiten my fingertips. "I'm fine." I let go of the table and picked up a pencil. "Just sleep-deprived."

"Maybe *you* need to do a bunch of mood-altering drugs," Jake said.

He wasn't entirely wrong.

After school, Kyla and Tess found me on my way to the parking lot and asked if I wanted to go to the mall. Of course I couldn't go, not with tomorrow's government/bio double whammy, but Rina could. I'd just have to make extra sure to get a full report.

"Wanna go shopping?" I called up to Rina as I walked in the front door. "Kyla went home to change, but she and Tess are gonna be here any minute to pick you up." Rina sprinted downstairs and predictably flipped out ("Shut up!

No! Really? Yes!") and I couldn't help but grin. Being able to do my work while not disappointing my friends and making Rina ridiculously happy felt amazing. She practically jumped up and down, took the money I gave her, then ran out the front door to wait for Kyla's car as I retired up to my room to tackle the remainder of this academic nightmare of a week.

Much later that night, after Rina had returned and carefully sneaked up to my room, I tapped on the closet door. Rina cracked it open and peeked out. "So did you have fun?" I asked

"Total fun," she answered, opening the door all the way and sitting down on the floor just inside the threshold. "Kyla's hilarious. Sometimes she talks so fast I don't even know what the hell happened—"

"I hear you on that," I said.

"—and Tess is really cool too. She looks like she could snap most people's necks. Do you think she could snap most people's necks?" Rina leaned back against the doorjamb, accidentally thumping her head. We both winced—sympathetically on my part.

"Probably," I admitted. Tess works out a lot and is also naturally built like a tank. "She wouldn't, but yeah, she definitely could," I agreed.

Rina nodded and didn't say anything.

"So what else did you guys talk about?" I asked. "Anything I need to be filled in on?" I didn't want to miss out on any gossip, and I especially didn't want to slip up on random information again.

"Not really," answered Rina. Her eyes flitted toward her sleeping bag and she picked up her pillow and hugged it to her chest.

"Oh, come on, you guys were out for like three hours— you had to have talked about something," I said. "Boys? Any new info on the Suarez situation?"

"Eh . . ." Rina mumbled, looking at her sleeping bag again. Was she being evasive on purpose? Or was she genuinely just really tired?

"Which stores did you go to?" I pressed, changing tacks. "Did you buy anything good?"

Rina shrugged. "It was just the normal places, you know . . . and I didn't see anything I liked, actually, so here's your money back." She reached into her pocket and handed me a crumpled twenty and a ten. I raised an eyebrow. I'd given her forty. "Oh, yeah, I almost forgot!" she said. "Here." Rina reached up and into the pocket of the coat she'd worn to the mall, and pulled out a little plastic case holding three lip glosses. "I thought you'd like these colors."

"Aww, thank you!" I said, opening the case and turning the gloss tubes over in my hand. I did like the colors. One was a shimmery beige, one a sort of silvery peach color, and the last was pink with very subtle gold flecks.

"You're welcome!" Rina said cheerfully. "I tried one on and it looked good on me, so I figured—"

"Of course," I said, grinning. "And you can borrow anytime."

"I was planning on it." Rina grinned back.

I half-successfully tried to stifle an oncoming yawn and then glanced over at the clock. It was past one. I shrugged. "Well, if you guys really didn't talk about anything else, I guess I'll just study some more. . . ." I didn't move toward my computer, waiting to see if Rina had anything to share.

"Yeah, totally," Rina agreed quickly. "Do you need help with anything?"

"Nah," I said. So much for giving her the third degree. I stood up and stretched, then paused before leaving the closet. "Do you want something to read in there?" I asked.

"No thanks," she answered, "I'm actually pretty zonked."

"Okay, good night," I said. But Rina had already curled up in her sleeping bag. She was out before I even finished shutting the door.

CHAPTER SIXTEEN
THURSDAY, DECEMBER 13

I POKED RINA AWAKE WITH MY FOOT. IT WAS rude, but I was trying to get my black cardigan sweater off the hanger above her head, and it had gotten snagged and required both my hands.

"Morning," she said finally, opening her eyes when my gentle foot-poking turned into near-kicks. "What's up? Did you want me to go to school for you?"

"No, I've still got finals," I said. "My last two, woo-hoo! But Paul has Spanish tomorrow and I promised I'd study with him, so I was wondering if you could—"

"Of course!" Rina said, wiggling out of her sleeping bag and leaping to her feet. I shushed her. My mom was still puttering around the house.

"Okay, can you hang with him in the library after school? I chose the location on purpose so we would definitely study, otherwise we might—"

Rina giggled.

"—get distracted," I finished lamely, blushing a little. "Anyway, after physics we'll switch behind school. Okay? Then you'll go back in and study with Paul, and I'll come home and work on my essay." Stupid essay. I figured I had a better chance of concentrating if I was home alone. But if there were any sort of unique life experience I should be writing about, having my identical twin come out of the computer and wreak havoc on everything she touched was kind of a no-brainer. Of course, that wasn't an option. At least not without Yale thinking I was crazy.

Although a crazy person would really round out their freshman class. . . .

With my luck, they'd probably already admitted one early.

"Got it," said Rina. She started looking around the closet, picking out an outfit.

"By the way," I added, "make sure to sit at one of the tables in the main room, not in a study room." I didn't need Paul having any excuse to get snuggly.

"Sure," Rina agreed. "But will Paul think it's weird that I'll need a ride home afterward? Since you're going to have the car?"

"Oh, good catch," I said. Damn logistical issues. "Um . . ."

"You know what? I'll just say Mom thought you looked too sleepy this morning to drive yourself."

"Perfect," I said. "Unfortunately, it's probably true. So . . . what should we wear?" If we were going to do this, I'd rather avoid stripping down in the parking lot. We both started trying to figure out what I had multiples of. In a sad commentary on the variety of my wardrobe, it actually wasn't that hard.

"Jeans and T-shirts it is," I said. We both pulled on jeans and a navy blue tee, and then I topped off my outfit with this really loud rainbow-colored argyle sweater my mom got for me a few years ago because she thought it was funny. As long as Rina put that on later, no one would question her identity. I pulled on sneakers, and she pulled on the older, more worn-out version that I still had lying around. We looked at ourselves in the mirror. Yep. Same person. Except for the sweater . . . and my visible exhaustion.

"Concealer?" Rina suggested. I sighed and took the tube she handed me.

After surviving my double final day, I escaped to the far corner of the parking lot, where the cement turned into the soccer fields and several large oak trees turned into the edge of the wooded nature center. A little farther back, a hiking trail curled around a well-hidden little duck pond. Rina stepped out from behind a tree just as I arrived.

"Here," I said, taking off the rainbow sweater.

"Coats," she reminded me, and I traded her my red winter coat for her black one. Then I followed from a distance as Rina walked back toward the edge of the woods, crossed the parking lot, and seamlessly blended in with the crowd of students heading toward their cars. If anyone had been stalking me, which they weren't, they would've seen me go into the woods for a bit, then stroll back out and return to school. Nothing suspicious there.

"Hey!" A thin blond figure waved at me from the parking lot. "Kate!"

My heart froze as I waved back at Anne from the edge of the woods. Oh God, she hadn't seen anything, had she?

"Hey," I said as I reached the parking lot. Her car was only a few spaces over from mine, and I wondered how long she'd been standing there.

"What's up?" she asked. "What were you doing out there?"

"Uh . . . cig break?" I asked, trying to sound jokey.

"You don't smoke," she pointed out. She lowered her voice conspiratorially. "Was Jake out there, too?"

My eyebrows shot up. "Huh?"

"I noticed you two having a private little convo in the hallway the other day, so I thought maybe—"

"What?" I choked out a totally not-suspicious laugh-cough. "Oh. *Nooooo*. I mean, yeah, I talked to him. But it was just physics stuff." So she hadn't seen Rina, but I was thoroughly annoyed at her implication. "There's nothing going on," I said firmly. "Nothing." I didn't want this line of questioning—or any other line, for that matter—to go further.

"Really?" Anne's face looked innocent, but her voice had a sharp edge. "Because you guys seem pretty friendly in class. And Paul's mentioned that you've been too busy to hang out with him lately, so—"

"That's totally not true," I snapped. "And I'm thrilled that Paul is talking to you about me, but it's really nothing you need to concern yourself with."

"Why wouldn't he mention it to me? He's my friend," Anne said sweetly.

"Well, he's *my* boyfriend," I shot back. I felt a smidge of satisfaction as anger flickered across her face, darkening her features.

"Of course he is," she answered evenly. Then she looked straight at me and added, "I don't want Paul to get hurt, and you've been acting kind of weird lately."

"Well, it's been a stressful week," I reminded her. "But it'll be worth it when I get into Yale. *With Paul.*" Anne's face went sour again, and I quickly faked a big, bright smile. "Anyway, see ya tomorrow!"

"Sure, see ya," she responded coolly. "Can't wait for

physics." She waved a little, then got in her car and drove off.

What the hell *was* that? I got in my car as well, feeling nauseated. Because she wasn't *totally* wrong—Rina *had* kissed Jake. And while she didn't have any actual evidence that I was cheating, I wouldn't put it past her to try to convince Paul anyway.

The idea made my skin crawl.

At home, my writer's block relented enough for me to string a few ideas together. The essay became a semi-snarky look at how much I'd kicked my own ass over the past four years. It was a typo-ridden jumble of half-formed thoughts, but I doubted anybody else's application contained the line "I'm so tired from high school that I might sleep my way through college (in the not-bothering-to-get-up-for-class way, not the sex way)." I patted myself on the back after I typed that, figuring that it at least qualified as "unique." Upon further reflection, I realized that it did not, however, qualify as "good."

Luckily, Rina came home that evening positively giddy. "He's so awesome, Kate, you are sooo lucky!" she squealed. She flitted around my room, yammering about how hot Paul was, how pretty his eyes were, how nice he was, and then some more about his hotness.

"I know, Rina," I said patiently. "He's my boyfriend. What'd you do, spend the whole time looking at him instead of studying?"

"What?" Rina asked. "It's not like *I* had to study. So yeah, maybe I glanced over a few times while I was pretending to work. Did you know that he does this thing where he leans back and stretches and then you can totally see his abs?"

"Yes, I knew that," I said. Paul does it all the time, inadvertently displaying his six-pack to distracting effect.

"It's awesome," Rina said, shaking her head in disbelief. "The abs look awesome."

"I'm glad you think so," I said, smiling at her and then looking back at my computer monitor, "because they feel even better."

"Dammit, I knew you were going to say that." Rina fake-pouted at me and I laughed. I liked hearing her gush over my boyfriend, although a tiny part of me wondered if I should be jealous that she'd spent all afternoon with him. Should I be annoyed? Or was I just the coolest, most un-neurotic girlfriend in the world? Hey, it wasn't like he was with some random. He was with, well, not me exactly, but my double. Wasn't that kind of the same thing?

Either way, I didn't have time to overanalyze.

"Well," Rina said dreamily, "I hope that Paul played SimuLife once too and his twin is about to arrive any day."

"Yeah, I'm gonna hope against that," I said dryly. "No offense."

"Some taken."

"Shut up."

"Okay."

I faux-glared at her. She faux-glared back.

We both giggled.

TO-DO LIST:
PRIORITY/ADDITIONAL

- Finals: ~~English take-home, French, Euro, bio, govt~~ DONE! Yay!
- Physics project ☹
- SATs ☹ ☹
- ESSAY ☹ ☹ ☹ (Have Paul write for me? Yeah, right. Argh.)
- Packing list for Yale (jeans, shirts/bras/undies, socks!
  Cardigan sweater, jacket? Going-out clothes?)
- Car: gas, check tire pressure, etc.
- Directions! Print map! Also schedule Sunday campus visit
  w/ host students, Monday interview, Tuesday bookstore/
  exploring/shopping/whatev
- Cash from Mom
- Google parking in New Haven—structures? Maybe call
  admissions office to see? You suck for not figuring this out
  before. What the hell is wrong with you?
- Beat Anne to pulp. Just kidding. Sort of.

CHAPTER SEVENTEEN
FRIDAY, DECEMBER 14

"CAN WE NAME OUR ROBOT DOUCHEBAG?"
Jake asked.

"I don't see why not," I said. "I certainly resent him enough at this point."

Jake and I were sitting in physics lab Friday afternoon, putting—hopefully—the final touches on our robot. We had until five p.m., but if all went well it would take only until the end of class. A few people had already turned their projects in and were playing with their phones, reading, or otherwise running out the clock until the end of the hour (and the semester). Lucky bastards. Anne casually walked around the classroom, ostensibly making small talk with other early finishers but somehow keeping close enough to our lab table to overhear what Jake and I were saying. It was irritating, to say the least.

"Okay, try it out," Jake said. He put a Ping-Pong ball

in the middle of the table while I positioned Douchebag at the table's edge. I pressed the button on the remote control. Douchebag rolled toward the Ping-Pong ball, picked it up, and . . . sat still.

"Dammit," Jake muttered.

"Ugh," I agreed. Douchebag was supposed to throw the Ping-Pong ball at three different targets, which were on a piece of posterboard set up next to the table, but instead he just held the ball in his little metal claw. I took the ball out and turned to Jake. "Now what?"

"I don't know, try one of the other settings," he said. We tried again. Douchebag successfully chucked the ball at the second target, but failed on the third one.

"Well . . . one out of three ain't bad." Jake stretched his arms behind his back and yawned.

"Yes it is," I said. "One out of three isn't an A. One out of three is, like, one-third credit."

"Quit exaggerating. It's more than that. We did the whole write-up." Jake fiddled with Douchebag's claw. It made a worrisome clicking noise. What the hell was wrong with it?

With fifteen minutes until the end of class, everyone was done except for us and Haylie Harmon and Jay Trale, who were over in the corner. "No," I said to Jake. "We can't turn it in like this."

"Oh, come on," Jake said. "It's close enough."

"No, you come on," I snapped. "What were you planning on doing after school?"

Jake shrugged. "Going home and starting my winter vacation." He smiled. "Probably playing Call of Duty until I can't see straight."

"Sorry, but I don't find Call of Duty a particularly convincing reason to stop working now." I looked at the clock again and winced when I heard a cheer from Haylie and Jay. Their mousetrap car had apparently just hit the target speed.

Jake rolled his eyes. "It's *sort* of working," he argued again. "We'd probably get a B. Can't you live with a B?" He idly punched the button on Douchebag's remote again. This time, the robot made a weird noise and didn't move at all.

"Oops," Jake said. I glared at him.

"Fine, we're staying." He sighed. He picked up the robot as the bell rang. Everyone else raced to the door amid chatter and cheers, Anne lingering just long enough to register that Jake and I were still there. She looked appraisingly at Jake, then smiled at me condescendingly and walked out the door. God. Dammit. But I had bigger worries at the moment.

"Um, Mr. Piper?" I walked to the front of the classroom to explain our situation.

"You have until five," he pointed out.

"I know," I said, "but that's only two hours from now, and this thing that was working before isn't working anymore. So if there's any way we could possibly get an extension, like maybe until—" I could hear my voice speeding up and my fingers clenched nervously.

"Kate, I know you're a responsible student," Mr. Piper said, noticing my growing panic. His voice turned more soothing. "Don't worry about it. I'll give you the rest of tonight; just leave your project here and I'll pick it up tomorrow morning at nine."

My eyes widened. "Oh my God, thank you! Thank you so much!"

"You're welcome. Have a good winter break." Mr. Piper threw some papers into his briefcase, snapped it shut, and left the room. I whooped to myself and turned to Jake, who was standing by our lab table, arms crossed, with a very sour look on his face.

"Okay, I just got us a massive extension, so I don't know why you look like that."

"Exactly," Jake answered. "Now we know we have all night. So it's probably going to actually take us all night."

"Wrong," I countered. "I have the SATs tomorrow morning. Obviously I don't want it to take that long. We'll get it done when we get it done, and we'll go faster if you quit complaining and start working." I picked up a pencil and then put it down again. "Oh, wait. I have to make a phone call." Jake rolled his eyes as I stepped out into the now-deserted hallway to call Paul.

Paul picked up on the first ring. "Hey, where are you?" he asked.

"Still at school," I told him. "Our robot malfunctioned and now we're trying to fix it."

"Ugh, sorry about that," Paul said sympathetically. "We're still hanging out later though, right?" We'd planned to repeat our pre-SAT (and PSAT and ACT) tradition: chill out, see a movie, not think about anything, and go to bed early.

"About that . . ." I started slowly, waiting for Paul's reaction. There was silence on the other end of the line. "I'm gonna try and get it done in the next few hours," I continued, "but just in case I don't—"

"Kate." Paul was clearly annoyed.

"What?" I asked.

"You're the one who was all gung-ho about relaxing before the SATs, and now you're bailing?"

"I'm not bailing," I said defensively. "I can't help that the thing malfunctioned." I glanced through the physics room window at Jake, who was looking intently at a calculator. "We're going to finish as soon as possible and then you and I can hang out." I tried to sound gentle and calm, but failed miserably. I hoped that Paul didn't notice my impatience.

He noticed. "Oh, so now *you're* mad at *me*?"

"I'm not mad," I said. "And you shouldn't be either.

I'm just trying to get this A so I have the best chance of getting into—"

"Yeah, yeah, getting into Yale with me," Paul interrupted, and I could tell he was rolling his eyes. "You know, it's kind of pointless if you're just gonna be like this next year."

"Like what?!" I exclaimed. "It's not my fault I have to stay here and—"

"It *is* your fault," snapped Paul. He officially sounded angry. "You and your slacker partner. I know you guys have been wasting time. Anne told me how much *fun* you guys have been having in class—"

"Okay, first of all, I can't believe you'd listen to her over me. You realize she still totally wants you and therefore she hates me, right?"

"—so what am I supposed to think when suddenly you're *supposed* to be done but somehow *magically* you're not—"

"She's totally exaggerating! I can't believe you're buying it."

"I mean, come on, you guys have been working on that stupid robot *forever* and you still can't get it to work—"

"If you think it's so easy then why don't *you* come over and—"

"—and now *I'm* the one paying for it? I mean, you *say* you're gonna try to hang out tonight. But I don't believe you." He practically spat those last couple words.

I was shocked at how furious he'd gotten and how quickly he'd gotten there. I could almost hear him clenching his phone in his fist. I knew I was clenching mine.

But he was right not to believe me. Even if this only took a few hours, I wasn't going to want to do anything but go to sleep when I was done building this damn robot.

"Paul," I pleaded quietly. I'd never heard him this angry—at me, at least. "I *promise* I'll finish in time for the movie, okay? I *swear.*"

There was a long, long silence. "Fine. What time should I pick you up?" His voice was cold.

Hmmm. I had no idea what time. "Um . . . eight?" I ventured. That gave me and Jake a little over four hours. If we didn't finish by then, I could send Rina. But four hours seemed doable.

"I'll come by your house," Paul said. His voice was completely flat, which was actually scarier than angry.

"Thanks," I said softly.

"I just don't know how you were so chilled out yesterday and today you're all nuts again—"

"What are you talking about?" Oh God. *Rina.* She'd hung out with him all afternoon. Great. They were supposed to have been studying, but apparently she'd been two tons of fun. "Um . . ." I tried to think of how to cover having no idea what Paul and Rina had talked about yesterday. I settled for rampant cheerfulness. "Well, whatever, don't worry. We'll have fun tonight, I promise! Okay?" I faked a smile, as if he could see it over the phone.

"Okay." Paul didn't sound convinced. "See you in a while." After he hung up, I sat listening to the silence. Now what? I could try *really* hard to finish the robot in the next few hours . . . but if that didn't happen . . . would I call it a night and risk a B, thereby sacrificing my entire future? Or would I cancel on Paul at the last minute and risk whatever that might do to his already brewing anger?

Forget it. Rina was going to the movies tonight and that was that.

I dialed my home number. The answering machine got it, just like it was supposed to whenever Rina was home alone. "Hey, it's me," I said. "Pick up the phone, will you? Hello? Hello? Helloooooo . . ."

"Hi!" Rina's voice was breathless. "What's up?"

"A bunch of stuff." I explained the situation as quickly as I could, although by the time the words "movie with Paul" came out of my mouth I could hear her footsteps pounding either down or up the stairs.

"Yes! Thank you!" she squealed. "Thank you thank you thank you! Oh my God, I have to decide what to wear!"

"Well, you've got a while to figure it out," I said. "Just make sure to come straight home afterward, and look to see if my bedroom light is on, since I have no idea what time we'll be done with our robot."

"Of course," Rina answered distractedly. "Thank you!" I heard the sound of hangers sliding across metal and realized that she must be in my closet. It was weird to think of her going through *my* clothes in preparation for a date with *my* boyfriend (especially when she asked if she could wear the black and silver—and extremely low-cut—tank top Kyla had loaned me), but whatever. It bought me time. And right now, that was all that mattered.

I went back to the physics lab. Now that it was pitch dark outside, we were practically the only people in the whole building. Every once in a while a janitor cart rolled by, and there were several minutes where we had to yell over the sound of a vacuum cleaner in the hallway, but other than that, it was silent. By ten o'clock, the robot was still just two for three on the targets.

"We're taking a break," I announced.

"Thank Christ," Jake answered immediately. He sprawled across one of the other lab tables facedown, resting his head on one wiry, flannel-shirted arm and letting the other one dangle toward the floor. I headed for the vending machine in the hall and got us both Diet Cokes, plus an assortment of Cheetos, SunChips, and mini-Oreos.

I returned to find Jake in the same position I'd left him in. "You asleep?"

"Yes," he answered, his voice muffled. "Wake me when it's all over."

I perched on the end of the table he was lying on and opened a Diet Coke. He perked up at the sound. I handed him a can, then put all the snack bags down.

"Hey, my favorite," he said, choosing the Flaming Hot Cheetos over the regular ones. "You remembered."

"Of course I did," I said. "How could I forget the red powder all over your video game controllers?"

"And the TV remote," he added.

"And everything else."

We kind of laugh-smiled at each other for a second, then swooped in on the food.

"So," Jake said, ripping the corner off the Cheetos bag, "what happens after we get our A on this thing?" He nodded toward the robot.

"*If* we get an A," I corrected, tearing into the Oreos.

"No way," he said. "The only reason we're still here is that precious A of yours. Otherwise I'd be in front of my Xbox right now. Killing. Or being killed. Hopefully killing, though."

"Fine," I replied, dangling my feet off the edge of the lab table. "When we get our A, knock on wood, I should have straight A's for the semester."

"And then what?" Jake asked.

"And then," I said, "tomorrow I will kick ass on my SAT retake. And then I will kick ass at my on-campus interview, and I'll get into Yale. And I will get to go to an awesome school and make my mom proud and just generally win at life. Duh." I grinned at him and playfully kicked him with my toe.

"Really?" Jake raised an eyebrow and stared at me, crunching on a Cheeto.

"What?" I asked.

Jake rolled his eyes very slightly, but I still noticed. "I don't know that what you just described qualifies as winning at life," he said. "Admit it. You only want to go to Yale because your boyfriend's going there."

"No," I said. "Of course not. I'm applying to all the Ivies. Yale's my top choice, but Paul's not the only reason."

"What're the other reasons? Actually, never mind, don't bother."

"What? I can list them. Um . . . because Harvard is too close to home. . . ." I paused. Jake didn't try to hide his eye roll this time. "Forget it," I snapped. He was clearly looking to shoot down my answers.

"How come you're so hard core about the Ivies, anyway?" he asked, tilting his head and looking at me.

"Because you're supposed to be!" I exclaimed. I was starting to feel like we were in an interrogation room. Next, Jake would be pacing back and forth playing both good cop and bad cop. "Doesn't everyone—"

"No, not everyone."

"Yeah, but I mean, if I want to go to grad school, or law

school or something, it would help if I went to a kick-ass college." There. That reason was bulletproof.

Jake raised an eyebrow. "That's it?"

"Are you kidding? That's huge," I said. I crumpled up the Oreo bag and walked toward the corner of the room to chuck it in the trash.

"You know what, forget it," Jake said. "It's not like it matters."

"Then why'd you bother asking?" I snapped. What was the deal with him passive-aggressively ripping on my future?

"I don't know," he answered with a shrug. "I guess I just wanted to see if . . ." He stared into space, zoned out for a second, and then snapped back to attention. "It's not important. We should get back to work."

"But—"

"Back to work, Miss Rina," Jake said in a mock stern voice.

"*WHAT*?!"

Jake laughed as my eyeballs threatened to liberate themselves from their sockets. "Hey, you were the one who renamed yourself for a month in eighth grade, remember? Something about it being a cooler nickname than Kate?"

"Oh," I said, nearly collapsing with relief. "Right."

"Or I guess it was Katie back then," Jake continued. "So back to work, Miss Katie." He smiled, dusted red powder off his hands, and went back to our lab table. I stared at him for a moment. No one had called me Katie since we were kids. Where was all of this coming from? And why was it bothering me so much?

But he was absolutely right about one thing. We'd already taken too long a break.

"Do you care if I play music?" Jake asked as I leaned down to inspect Douchebag. I shook my head. He started the MP3 player on his phone, and for the next half hour we worked to the sounds of Pink Floyd, the Beatles, Led Zeppelin, and for some reason the sound track to *Wicked*.

"Shut up," Jake said, when I gave him a look. "My mom borrowed my computer and the phone somehow sucked that on there, and I haven't figured out how to take it off yet."

"Hey, I didn't say anything," I laughed. "Feel free to enjoy your show tunes." I paused for a beat. "I mean, I think it's great that you're actually a twelve-year-old girl. . . ."

Jake reached over and hit his phone. The song switched from *Wicked* to the *Legally Blonde* sound track. Jake sighed as I smirked at him. "My mom's not gonna hear the end of this," he muttered, before hitting the phone again, and swearing when "One Day More" from *Les Mis* started playing.

"I actually like that song."

"Yeah, me too," Jake said with a small smile. "I take

full responsibility for that one." But he'd already hit the phone again. "Sabotage" by the Beastie Boys started, and Jake gave me a sort of triumphant "*now* are you happy?" look. I smiled, nodding and fake-dancing for a second as he fiddled with one of the robot's arms. Two of the three trajectories had each worked ten times in a row and we just needed the third.

"Okay. Let's try it," Jake declared. He picked up one of our Ping-Pong balls from the floor and set it at the center of the table.

"Fingers crossed," I said. Jake crossed his right-hand fingers, then his left-hand fingers, then entwined his arms for good measure. I followed suit before hitting the remote control.

Douchebag rolled over to the Ping-Pong ball, picked it up, and threw it at target number three. Direct hit.

"Yes!" we both yelled, jumping up and throwing our arms in the air.

We attempted to high-five, half-missed each other in our excitement, then stumbled forward and hugged. Unfortunately, the image of Rina and Jake in my living room chose that moment to flood into my brain. I could feel myself blushing. From the look on his face, Jake remembered too, and we quickly stepped apart, both of us staring uncomfortably at the windows, the ceiling, the walls—anything but each other.

But the robot worked! We put another Ping-Pong ball in the center of the table and tested it again. Ten successful throws later, we were done and, with our kick-ass write-up, sure to get an A. *Thank God.* Jake and I both stared at the robot happily, breathing sighs of relief.

Finally Jake broke the silence. "We're still calling him Douchebag though, right?"

"Oh yeah," I said quickly.

Jake and I grinned at each other, put Douchebag and our lab report on Mr. Piper's desk, packed up our stuff, and walked out the door.

Dear Diary,

I just got back from my first official date.
I could get used to this.

Love, Rina

CHAPTER EIGHTEEN

BY THE TIME I GOT HOME FRIDAY NIGHT, MY mom had gone to bed and left me a note saying, "Good luck on SATs, fridge has waffles & PB." I might have missed my pretest relaxation with Paul, but at least Mom had remembered to stock my favorite breakfast. Having eaten vending machine junk food for dinner, I made myself a waffle and took it up to my room.

"I beat Mom home, but just barely," Rina whispered when I came in. She'd already been hiding out in my closet for a while. She was wearing pajamas and sat curled up on her sleeping bag with the last Harry Potter book.

"Cool," I whispered back. "I'm going to bed. Tell me about you and Paul and the movie tomorrow, okay? Everything's fine with him, right? He's not mad at me anymore?"

"Nope, he's good," said Rina. "It was totally fun. By the way, last chance to have me take the SATs for you."

I stuck my tongue out at her.

"Had to try." She smiled. "I even studied, just in case." She moved the Harry Potter aside to show that she had a few of my SAT practice books in the sleeping bag with her. I shook my head disbelievingly as she grinned and closed the closet door.

When my alarm clock rang the next morning, I almost took her up on her offer. The last thing I wanted to do was leave the cozy warmth of my soft flannel sheets to drive through the cold to fill in little circles for hours—again. By the time I finally forced my eyes open, Rina was already dressed and waggling a handful of number two pencils at me. It was very tempting. But having her help me out with schoolwork and certain aspects of my social life was one (already somewhat shady) thing. Having her cheat for me on a national exam was entirely different, and entirely not cool. And possibly illegal—not that I had any idea what the criminal punishment for something like that would be.

So I sucked it up, got dressed, stuffed my face with coffee and peanut butter waffles, and drove to school. After all, this time I knew exactly what to expect, from the slightly too-warm testing room (a blocked-off section of the auditorium) that had me stripped down to my tank top by the third section, to asking for one of those wooden boards they give left-handers even though I'm not left-handed, because it expanded the surface area of my tiny little foldout desk.

I sailed through all the sections, and by the end I was pretty sure that I'd beaten my last score (as long as I didn't get totally screwed over by whoever was judging the essay). I looked at the clock. Four minutes left and it would all be over. Hell, it was already sort of over, but I started checking my answers anyway.

And suddenly, it hit me. My essay topic. I knew what I was going to write. The words sprang clearly into my head, almost as if the thing had written itself already and was just waiting for me to transcribe it onto the computer. *Finally.* I actually couldn't wait to start typing.

After I turned in my booklet and gathered up my stuff, I texted Mom that I was going to go work at Starbucks, and called Paul and told him the same thing. They both wished me luck with the writing. Paul added that he couldn't wait until I hit "send" on that application at midnight so he could finally have his girlfriend back.

"We hung out last night!" I pointed out, then immediately wished I hadn't. I had no idea what had gone on during the movie date. Paul and I weren't fighting anymore, but what had he and Rina talked about? I didn't even know what movie they'd gone to see. So much for due diligence.

"Yes, and it only makes me want more," Paul replied. "So hell yeah, forgive me if I'm doing a countdown."

"Okay," I said. "Count away. I'll call you if I finish early."

I hung up, returned the high-five of a random kid who was high-fiving everyone on his way out of the building, and drove home to get my laptop. I told Rina where I was going and asked her to lie low all day.

The blast of freezing cold air that hit me as I walked from my parking space to the door of Starbucks helped wake me up. I bought a venti vanilla latte to stave off the test-taking adrenaline crash I felt coming on and settled in at a large table in the back corner. Then, finally, I started typing.

It's not like I'm a split personality or anything.

Right?

I chugged some coffee. I wrote about how there had essentially been two versions of me over the past several years—the super-hardworking girl doing everything in her power to get into college, and then the totally exhausted kid underneath. I wrote about how the driven, Ivy-bound me had gradually taken over as I'd gotten older, had pushed the carefree me out of the way. I knew what I wanted and was working to get it. But it had a cost, paid with a skipped party here and a bailed-on movie there, and dozens of very un-lazy Sunday afternoons. I wrote about building the robot, how two different working styles had clashed, yet made something worthwhile. The two sides of my personality were

similarly battling it out: the lighthearted kid had been buried by the worker bee, but was beginning to claw to the surface. I didn't know if any of this was what Yale was looking
for, but it was a straightforward and honest record of my
high school experience. And that would have to do.

The afternoon stretched into evening. I wrote and
rewrote, trying to figure out the best balance between super
serious and kind of humorous, then just writing what felt
natural. I fixed typos. I rewrote some more. And finally, I
typed the last few words:

> . . . and so, after all this time, I'm a split personality no longer.
>
> Yes you are.
>
> No I'm not.
>
> Yes, you are.
>
> NO, I'M NOT. . . .

That was it. I paused thoughtfully for a moment, and
then scrolled back up to the beginning to look the whole
thing over. Was it unique enough? Was it well written and
captivating and all the things it was supposed to be? Would
it draw the readers in? And then hold on to them? Most
importantly, would it get me into Yale?

Stop psyching yourself out. This was it. This was the
essay. It was infinitely better than all my previous half-
baked ideas, and I'd truly felt inspired. If that wasn't good
enough, well . . . I didn't really want to think about it.

I saved the file and e-mailed it to myself as a backup. I chucked my fifth coffee cup into the trash and headed outside, walking toward my car with a sense of triumphant calm.

All I had to do was get home, attach my essay to my application, send the whole thing in, and I would be done. Free. Well, free to drive to New Haven tomorrow for my interview, but I wasn't worried about that anymore. I just had to show up and not do anything stupid (which would be easy, as I wasn't planning on dropping acid with my host students or entering amateur night at a New Haven strip joint). I pumped up the radio on the way home, laughing when I heard a commercial for the touring production of *Wicked* as I remembered the look on Jake's face when the sound track had come blaring out of his phone last night.

Then I turned the corner toward my house and abruptly stopped laughing. I also abruptly stopped driving, slamming on my brakes in the middle of the street.

There were two people on my front porch. Even at a distance, I recognized Paul and Rina. And even at a distance, I saw that they were kissing.

I stopped breathing. This wasn't happening. I was hallucinating again, right? I willed the image on the porch to go blurry and rearrange itself into something normal, something decent, something not completely nightmarish.

It was impossible to believe that this could actually be real.

But they kept kissing, her arms around his waist, his fingers twined in her hair. And then Rina took Paul's hand, opened the door, and led him into the house.

What.

The.

F?!

CHAPTER NINETEEN

IT TOOK ALL OF MY STRENGTH NOT TO FLOOR the car toward the porch, ram it through my front door, and run over them both. I tightened my hands on the steering wheel until I could feel my fingers getting numb from lack of blood, then screamed. Flat-out screamed. My windows were rolled up and nobody on the street had their house windows open, so I doubted anyone could hear me. But if they had, they would've heard the sound of fury mixed with . . . well, more fury. Sprinkled with some anger, swirled in with a dollop of murderous intent, and topped off with a healthy dose of rage.

But there was nothing I could do. Running through the front door and kicking everyone's ass was a delightful thought, but not an option without dragging Paul into the madness of the past two weeks. I took a few deep breaths to calm down (it didn't work), then parked my car at the curb. I walked over to my garage door and peeked in the window—my mom's car wasn't in there. Great. Just great. Paul and Rina were *alone* in my house.

I wiped away the tears of anger that had somehow trickled down my face without my noticing and semi-stealthily walked around the outside of my house. The curtains were all pulled, and the only lights on were in the downstairs hall and my bedroom. Oh my God, they were in my room! My evil twin was in my room with my boyfriend, while I was trapped outside my own house, in the cold and the dark.

"Wow, it's the best day ever," I said out loud, my voice cracking with hysteria. Where was my mom? Where the hell was my mom? I texted her. She was at work, of course, and texted back that she was going to have a late night prepping to go to Kansas City tomorrow. Great. I'd forgotten about my mom's business trip this week, but I bet Rina hadn't. I bet this was part of her master plan. But while my mom leaving town tomorrow was bad, what was happening right now was worse. There they were, in my room together, and my mom wouldn't be home for hours.

Wait a minute.

My mom wouldn't be home for hours, but I could make it sound like she was.

Duh! I sprinted to my car, fired up the engine, and drove into my garage, smiling as the garage door clanged on its cold hinges. As I cracked open the door leading into the house, I saw Paul coming down the stairs, followed by Rina.

"Are you sure I shouldn't say hi to your mom?" he was asking, his fingertips lightly twined with hers. Ugh.

"No, she's probably zonked from work," said Rina, "and it's not like she hasn't said hi to you before." She smiled, all flirty and playful, and I almost threw up. When he bent his head to kiss her, I actually gagged, holding my hand over my mouth to muffle the sound. Thankfully, he quickly slipped out the front door toward his car, because the rage in my stomach had traveled to my fists.

I stormed into the front hall and shoved Rina so hard she backed up a few steps and hit the wall. "You SLUT!"

Rina stumbled, surprised and off balance, but quickly recovered. "Kate, there you are! I'm sorry, but it's nothing, really. He just stopped by and—"

"You're *lying*!" I yelled. "My boyfriend cheated on me! With YOU!"

"No," Rina said. "No, that's not what happened. I mean, obviously I had to pretend to be you and go along with—"

"You didn't *have* to do anything! What did you do, call him? I told him I was gonna be working all day. I told you that too, and you—" I couldn't believe how stupid I'd been. Suddenly I could see exactly what had happened. "You knew I was gonna be gone and you took advantage of it! What did you tell him? Did you say you finished the essay early? What the *hell* is wrong with you?"

Rina's expression changed. Her eyes went from wide-eyed and innocent to narrow and calculating. She gave me a tight little smile. "Fine," she said quietly. "You're right. That's exactly what I did. Happy?"

"No!" I couldn't believe what I was hearing. "No, I'm not happy! I won't be happy till you leave! Get out of here! I don't care where you go; I don't care what you do. I don't care if somebody finds you and we both get locked up. This is my life, not yours, so—"

"Oh, I'm not going anywhere," Rina said calmly. She walked over to the stairs, sat down, and looked up at me, her brown eyes unblinking.

"Except that you are," I said, grabbing her arm, and hauling her to a standing position.

"I don't think so." Rina shook me off. "I mean, you kind of owe me."

"I owe you? *I* owe *you*?" I shrieked.

"You wouldn't have gotten through this past week if it hadn't been for me," Rina retorted. "I went to class for you so you would have time to study. I made you flash cards and organized your notes. I woke you up when you fell asleep doing work. I took care of prom and yearbook stuff you were totally slacking on. I wrote your English final, for chrissakes."

"What are you talking about? I totally did that myself! You saw me typing it!"

"Yeah, well, you didn't see me switch it. With the one I wrote. Which was better."

My jaw fell open and I stared at her. "When did you—"

"Before you woke up. It's not like it was hard. A bomb could go off in that room and you wouldn't know it, you're so sleep-deprived." Rina rolled her eyes. "You're welcome, by the way. Mine got an A, and I'm sure yours would've gotten a B-plus at best. Your 4.1 would be shot to hell if you'd turned that thing in."

"I can't believe you did that," I said softly, backing away a little. "I didn't want . . . I never wanted—"

"Please," Rina scoffed. "You *so* did." She crossed her arms and stared at me. "I hung out with your friends because you asked me to. I hung out with Paul because *you asked*. He was mad at you for bailing on him all the time. He might've broken up with you by now if I hadn't been around to help." I winced, just barely, but she noticed it and smiled. "And *now* you're mad?" she asked. "Do you really think that's the first time he wanted to hook up with his girlfriend this week?"

My mouth fell open. Rina stared at me and I stared right back. She couldn't. . . . They hadn't. . . .

My legs suddenly felt like they were going to give out,

and I had to sit on the floor, leaning against the wall. Rina rolled her eyes and laughed. "I can't believe you fooled yourself for so long," she said, looking down at me, her voice mocking. "You are seriously delusional if you thought you could've made it through this past week without me, at least not without losing your precious class rank or getting, like, a 2 on the SATs. You're a mess. You're about one thread away from totally snapping, and you definitely would've if I hadn't shown up. I mean, look what time it is—you're about to miss the Yale deadline."

I looked at my watch and my eyes widened. *Eleven fifty-six.* My application was due at midnight. No. *No!* My wobbly legs were suddenly strengthened by adrenaline and panic. I sprinted up to my room, barely registering Rina behind me. I rushed to my computer, downloaded my essay from e-mail, and opened up my application. I tried to attach the essay, but the window froze. Dammit! It was now eleven fifty-nine. I tried again, shaking in fear that I wouldn't make it in time. Suddenly Rina's hand grabbed the mouse, moved it to the "send" button, and clicked.

"What did you just do?" I screeched.

"Sent my application to Yale," Rina said calmly. "Your essay wouldn't attach because I already attached mine. See?" She indicated an open document entitled "Crossed Country."

"What the hell is that?"

"Your college application essay," Rina answered. "Or rather, mine. Read it if you want. It's genius, if I do say so myself."

"What are you talking—"

"Please, I read that half page of notes you wrote the other day. They were pathetic. And I doubt the one you wrote today is any better. But mine? Mine's getting us in." She threw a triumphant look at the computer and then a scornful one back at me.

I stared at her, numb with shock. I had no idea what was going on anymore—I had no idea what to do or say. If it were possible, I would have forgotten to breathe and keeled over dead. And I think Rina knew it. She got up, went over to the mirror to fix her hair, and calmly kept talking. "Oh, and since I wrote the essay, I'll be the one driving to New Haven tomorrow for the on-campus interview. I'm pretty sure you'd just try too hard and screw it up." Rina glanced at me, then moved her eyes over to my jewelry box sitting on the dresser. She opened it, picked out some delicate gold vintage-style earrings that my mom had given me for my birthday, and put them on. She admired her own reflection. "So I'll be taking your car tomorrow," she continued. "And I'm also taking our favorite jeans."

I opened my mouth, but no words came out. Rina glanced back at me. "Don't look so surprised," she said lightly. "I got sick of waiting for you to help me figure out my life, that's all. But I guess that's not surprising, since you couldn't even handle yours."

We suddenly heard the sound of the garage door opening.

"Mom," I rasped, unable to make my voice any louder. I wasn't crying—not really—but my body was so tense I was surprised I hadn't shattered. "She's home," I tried again, my voice hoarse and tired and still much too quiet. "You can't—you have to—"

"Hey, I know the drill," Rina said. "Don't have to tell me twice." She smiled coolly and strolled over to the closet. "Night, sis," she singsonged, stepping inside and closing the door. "Wish me luck for tomorrow."

TO-DO LIST

*** KILL EVERYBODY (i.e., Rina)

CHAPTER TWENTY
SUNDAY, DECEMBER 16

AT FOUR IN THE MORNING, I STILL COULDN'T fall asleep, but it wasn't a tossing-and-turning sort of night. It was a lying-dead-still-not-even-bothering-to-close-my-eyes sort of night. What would've happened if I'd been nicer to her? (Except I *was* nice!) What if I'd just realized earlier that Rina was completely and totally evil? (Except she'd done such a good job pretending!) The closet was silent. I had no idea if she was asleep in there, or if she was mulling over her recent victories, or perhaps plotting something even more nefarious.

I stared at the ceiling. I had no idea how I was going to prevent her from going to my Yale interview for me.

Unless.

Unless I left now?

I sat straight up, kicking myself for not thinking of this before. Of course! I would just leave before she did! Okay, this was not a well-thought-out plan, but at least it was a plan. I swung my feet out from under the covers and quickly stood up, wincing as both my bed and a floorboard creaked. Almost instantly, the closet door cracked open.

"I heard that," murmured Rina's voice from the darkness, just loud enough for me to hear. "You're not exactly the queen of stealth." She flipped on the closet light, throwing a white-gold beam across the floor, then stuck her hand out the door, just far enough for me to see that she had my car keys in it. "I don't know what you're doing. But if you plan on going farther than the bathroom—like say, New Haven—you'll probably need these."

"Wrong," I hissed at her, "There's a spare set in the—" I stopped, realizing I had no idea where my mom kept my spare car keys.

"Kitchen drawer?" asked Rina innocently. She stuck her other hand out and I saw my spare keys dangling from her fingertips.

"What," I said, my voice a whisper of controlled anger, "is keeping me from wrestling those away from you right this second?"

"Fear," she answered matter-of-factly. "Because I would scream bloody murder, and your mom would hear." She shut the closet door and after a moment, the beam of light under it disappeared.

I got back in bed, cursing the world for having Rina in

it. Granted, maybe it was better if she left. At least then she'd be impersonating me to strangers in New Haven, instead of to people I knew at home. I resolved to stay awake, in case a brilliant solution hit me before the morning, and I sat up in bed, prepared to rack my brain until it did. But I hadn't had a full night's sleep in ages, and as dawn approached, my exhaustion got the better of me. I eventually drifted off into blackness—silent and devoid of dreams.

I slept for over ten hours. By the time I woke up, the house was empty. Mom was off on her business trip, and Rina had taken my car. She had also taken my backpack, my iPod, a bunch of clothes, and who knew what else, but I was delighted to the point of hysterics to find my cell phone buried under the covers of my bed. I hadn't hidden it deliberately (although, in retrospect, I should have), but if she'd taken it, she would surely be wreaking havoc on Paul, and maybe even my other friends, from out of town.

"Thank God," I said out loud, turning the phone over in my hands gratefully. I looked up at the ceiling and prayed briefly that Rina would somehow crash on the highway, and that the car would explode, burning away all the evidence.

Of course, that would leave me without a car.

I got up, my happiness fading and my daze of anger and confusion returning, and went downstairs to get something to eat. *There's always murder. It's not like anybody knows Rina exists, so as long as you hid the body properly . . .* Yeah, right. My town didn't exactly have a convenient water-filled gravel quarry to chuck a corpse into, and there was no way in hell I could dig a shovel far enough into the frozen ground to cover a whole person. I couldn't even believe my mind had wandered as far as that sort of technicality.

But what was I going to do? Rina wasn't going to murder me and then just live my life, was she?

Christ, was she?

That was ridiculous. I mean, the entire situation was out of control, but it wasn't a *horror* movie.

I hoped.

I poured myself a bowl of cereal and sat down at the kitchen table, idly using the back of my spoon to crunch the flakes down so that they were all below the milk line. Now what? I didn't have homework. There weren't any flash cards that needed memorizing or lab experiments to write up. For the first time in years, I had nothing to do. And I couldn't even enjoy it.

I took my cereal bowl back up to my room and sat down at my computer to check my e-mail. And there, on the computer desktop, I saw it. The icon for Rina's college essay.

I opened the file.

"Crossed Country"

AP bio, meet Kearney, Nebraska. Kearney, Nebraska, meet AP bio.

I had just found myself stranded by the side of the road.

Nebraska? What was she talking about? The essay was a chronicle of how Rina had apparently applied high school academics to surviving a solo cross-country road trip. Expectedly, but annoyingly, the thing was good. Hell, it was great—funny, but touching, easily weaving a high school career's worth of academic achievement with a lifetime's worth of street sense and wry wit. It was serious in parts and flippant in parts, but every single sentence sparkled with intelligence. Only it was all a lie—as *if* Rina had ever been on a road trip by herself! As *if* she'd used obscure knowledge from the AP chem test to help conjure a gasoline substitute when her car broke down in Tennessee! But the essay was believable—it was totally believable. And readable, and memorable, and oh-so-annoyingly unique.

It was way better than mine, and it was probably going to get me into Yale.

Or rather, her.

I resisted the urge to slam my head face-first into my desk. Rina had done me a favor by sending in that essay. Except that she hadn't meant to. She'd done *herself* a favor, unless I figured out some way to get rid of her. But assuming

I got in, I'd be going to Yale on the strength of something I hadn't written. This was exactly the scenario I'd wanted to avoid when Rina had first suggested doing my homework for me. I'd expected today to feel like a coronation—finally accomplishing everything I wanted. But this was exactly what I *didn't* want.

My phone rang. Paul.

I let it go to voice mail, not knowing what I might blurt out if I actually picked it up (perhaps something along the lines of "Hi, you don't know you suck, and it's not your fault you suck, but you still suck"), then listened to the message.

"Hey, it's me. Thought I might come over—call me back." Wait, what? He knew I was supposed to be out of town. I texted him back. I wanted to see him but didn't trust what I would say. Twenty minutes later, Paul was at my front door.

"Hi there," he said, grinning and bending down to give me a big hug.

"Hi," I said, reluctantly letting his strong arms squeeze me tightly. All I could think about was the sight of him and Rina together, and the memory made me dizzy. I closed my eyes for a moment, then finally mustered the willpower to arrange my face into a happy expression. Sort of. The smile I managed to paste on looked totally fake when I glimpsed myself in the mirror across from the coat closet, but Paul didn't seem to notice.

"So," he said, leaning toward me. "We've got the house to ourselves. . . ."

I backed away from him. "Yep. Mom's not here. True."

Paul tilted his head and gave me a weird look. "Is something wrong?"

"Well, yeah," I said. I headed for the stairs and started walking toward my room. "I'm supposed to be in New Haven right now, remember?" I couldn't believe that he'd forgotten my campus visit. I'd been giving him the benefit of the doubt earlier, figuring he'd just had a temporary brain freeze or gotten the date mixed up, but this was ridiculous.

Paul followed me into my room, sat down at the foot of the bed, and stared at me for a second, confused. "Oh, right," he said, shrugging out of his coat. "Right! I totally forgot! Wait, then why are you here?"

"I just—I don't really feel well, so I rescheduled," I said. I sat down next to him, pulling my knees up to my chest, and watched as he took off his baseball cap and ran his hand through his hair. "Yesterday was . . ." I paused, waiting to see whether he would say anything that would give me a clue as to what had gone on between him and Rina.

"Yesterday was what?" Paul asked. "Great? You seemed really good last night. When I left you were going to send in your application. You did turn it in, didn't you?"

"Yeah, I turned it in," I said, picturing Rina's hand clicking the mouse button for me. "I just . . ." I looked down at my bedspread and suddenly realized that the last time Paul had been in here, he'd been in here with *her*. I shivered, hopefully not noticeably, and scooched away from Paul a little bit.

"What's wrong?" he asked, the look on his face genuinely worried now, instead of just confused. "Did something happen?"

A lot of things happened, I thought to myself. *Way too many things.* "No, nothing happened," I said.

"Well, if nothing happened, why'd you reschedule?" Paul looked at me, his blue eyes skeptical. "Do you really think that's a good idea? I mean, I hope you at least *told* them you got majorly sick. If they think you're blowing them off, it might hurt your chances."

"Whatever." I scooched back a little more. His tone had gone from skeptical to disapproving, which was irritating. "I just rescheduled for next month. It's not that big a deal."

"Okay, okay," he said, hearing my defensiveness and backing off. He half-smiled. "Wow, did you get hit in the head or something? You've been so psyched about this interview forever."

"No," I answered, feeling a glimmer of hope. "Why, have I been acting like I got hit in the head?" Had he noticed that he'd been with an entirely different girl the past few days? If he'd noticed, then . . . well, I didn't know what, but I did know that I wanted him to have noticed.

"No," Paul answered. "It was just a joke."

Oh.

"So I haven't been acting different lately?" I asked him hopefully. I didn't really care that the question came out of nowhere. This conversation was already spiraling down-ward. No sense trying to steer it back. The brake lines were cut; the car was heading off the cliff.

"No," Paul said, shrugging. "Same old you. Although you're acting kind of weird right *now*."

"What's that mean?" I crossed my arms and backed away a little more. I was now sitting kind of far away from him, actually, almost on my pillow at the head of the bed. I watched as he realized it too, and gave me an odd look.

"I don't know, the last couple days you were so fun and sort of, you know, carefree—"

"I was?"

"—and now we're on vacation and finals are over, so you'd think now you'd be chilled out. But instead you're act-ing extra crazy."

"Am not," I retorted like a four-year-old.

"You just postponed your interview. That's a *little* crazy." Paul gave me a look like he expected me to agree. "And quit getting mad, I'm just trying to help. I just want you to get in."

"What for?" I asked. "So I can follow you all over campus next year?" My voice had gotten shrill without me even realizing it.

"Of course," Paul joked, then, noticing my daggerlike stare, shook his head. "No," he said. "I want you to get in because that's what *you* want."

I stared at him, unable to answer for a long moment. "Yeah," I said finally. "Right." Of course that's what I wanted. To go to an Ivy League school, preferably the one my boyfriend was at. What could be better? It was the *plan*.

"Okay then," he said.

We were both quiet for a long moment. Paul stared into space. I stared at the floor. Finally, Paul broke the silence. "Should I just leave?" he asked.

"I guess," I agreed flatly. Out of the corner of my eye, I saw him look over at me, but I kept staring at the floor, clutching my pillow.

"Fine." Paul got up, and I blinked back a tear. How had this turned into a fight? No, I knew how. And I knew that I'd done it, but I desperately wished that I hadn't. I wanted to rewind our conversation and start over. Paul saw the look on my face and his expression softened. "Hey," he said. "It'll be okay. I'm sorry—you're just having a bad day."

I clutched my pillow harder and nodded, willing the tears not to fall.

"I'll leave you alone," Paul said softly. "Is that okay? Or did you want me to stay?" He took a step back toward me.

I shook my head and he sighed. "Okay. I'll see you later." He turned to leave, and a few moments later I heard him drive off.

I was alone again.

I got up, walked to my window, and stared out into the pitch-dark late afternoon. The day had ended as badly as it had begun, and Rina wasn't even around. But as I noticed a few tiny sprinkles of snow beginning to fall, I realized that she'd been right. She'd picked up my slack. She'd made it possible for me to do multiple things at once. Who knows what would've happened if she had never shown up? I might've stressed out and flunked all my finals. I might've lost so much sleep that I keeled over during the SATs.

And if I got into Yale based on her essay, that meant I probably couldn't have done that without her either. She was the same person I was, sure, but the smarter and more efficient version (and the more evil version, but that was a side issue). She was the better version.

So what did that say about me?

I'd been awake for barely half a day, but I hit the lights and crawled back into bed.

CHAPTER TWENTY-ONE
MONDAY, DECEMBER 17

AFTER SLEEPING FOR ANOTHER ELEVEN HOURS straight (boy, I really *was* sleep-deprived), I got up determined to do something productive with my Monday. Namely, to stop moping, take advantage of the fact that Rina was gone, and figure out a way to get rid of her once and for all. I didn't care if I had to go to the library to look up books on witchcraft and cast some sort of disappearing spell by the light of the silvery moon. I didn't even care if that disappearing spell involved an animal sacrifice, as long as it wasn't anything too fluffy and cute.

But first, I needed coffee.

I went downstairs to the kitchen and glanced at the empty French press. *Nope. Starbucks it is.* My workout regimen had been nonexistent as of late, so I changed into running clothes and sprinted out into the cold. The snow that I'd seen falling last night had settled into a thin layer of white frost on the ground, and the icy air washed past my face, shocking me awake and clearing my head.

My feet pounded the sidewalk as I headed for Starbucks and mentally formulated a plan. First, I would look on the Internet again for an old SimuLife disk. If that didn't pan out—and I didn't have high hopes that it would—I would call the company that designed the game to see if there was any back stock in a storage warehouse somewhere. Beyond that, I didn't really have any ideas. But at least I was caffeinated now, walking briskly toward home with a steaming-hot mocha warming my hands.

A car horn honked behind me. I turned around to see Jake idling in the middle of the street. He was wearing a thick winter coat and a blue fleece hat. He had apparently had a coffee craving as well, judging from the cup he was sipping from with one hand as the other rested on the steering wheel.

"You. Need a ride home," he said, grinning.

"Need? No," I said, blushing slightly at my post-run sweatiness. "Will accept? Yes." I walked toward his passenger-side door as he reached across and opened it for me. A few minutes later we were in my driveway.

"You wanna come in?" I asked.

"That depends on whether your kitchen has breakfast foods."

"It does."

"Then yes." Jake grabbed my physics notebook from the backseat. "Here, by the way. It got stuck with some of my stuff in lab the other day."

"Oh, thanks," I said, taking it as he followed me into my kitchen. He shrugged out of his coat and took off his hat, which had given his short black hair the faintest hathead. He realized this when I smirked at him, and quickly ran his hand over his head to fix it.

I took off my fleece and warmed up some frozen waffles, then settled into the chair across from him. "I may burn this," I said, plunking the physics notebook onto the table.

"Don't you need it for second semester?"

"Okay, fine, I guess I won't burn it." I looked at the cover, where Jake had drawn a cartoon version of me beating our stupid robot to death with a baseball bat. I laughed. "Nice work."

"Thanks," he answered. "Originally it was going to be both of us beating him to death, but I think you were the one with more resentment by the end. Plus my pencil broke."

I laughed again. "By the way, what the hell are you doing up so early?"

"Haven't been to bed yet," Jake said cheerfully, and I suddenly realized how tired he looked. His brown eyes were shadowed, and his angular face was pale. "Told you, as soon as we finished that robot I got started on Call of Duty, so my sleep schedule's all screwed up. You, on the other hand, look totally awake. For the first time in . . . ever."

"Are you saying I looked bad before?" I asked.

"Yes," he answered simply, then grinned as I kicked him under the table. He took a huge swig of coffee. "Now my turn to ask a question—why are you even home? Aren't you supposed to be at Yale?"

Oh, right.

"Yeah," I said glumly, taking a sip of coffee. "I canceled, though. Things have been sort of . . . weird lately."

"Yeah, I noticed," Jake said.

He'd noticed?

I looked up at him and he kept talking. "Not to bring up a subject you said was dead, but ever since last week . . ."

Right, the kiss. I shuddered inwardly.

". . . it's like . . . sometimes you acted one way and sometimes you acted another way, and it was all you, but it also, like, wasn't. If that makes any sense." Jake half-shrugged and took another swig of coffee, the cup obscuring his face so I couldn't quite read his expression.

My eyes widened. If only he knew how much sense it made.

"Yeah, so . . . anyway," Jake said, putting his cup down. He looked a little embarrassed at having brought up the subject. His face was tentative, and the tips of his ears were pink. I nodded, partly for encouragement and partly because I was dying to know what he was about to say. "So, um, last week when I was here . . ." he continued.

"Yeah . . ." I said, trying to keep my voice neutral. But I couldn't help leaning forward a little.

"You were really nice and that was, I mean it was great, but it was also weird, and then when we, you know . . ."

I winced.

He stopped talking. "Sorry."

"No, no, keep going. I just feel bad about the whole—"

"Yeah, see, that's the thing," he said. He picked up his hat, which was lying on the chair next to him, and started fidgeting with it. "That day, in your living room, you totally didn't seem like you felt bad, even though knowing you, you *would* feel bad. But then later at school you felt terrible. I could tell it was killing you."

I nodded, feeling a tiny flutter of hope.

"You were way more normal at school than you were here, for some reason," Jake continued. "So it was all just . . ."

"Weird," I finished. Again, he had no idea how accurate his assessment was.

"Very weird," he agreed, putting the hat down and picking up his coffee again. "No offense."

"Yeah, no . . ." I said, trailing off. "None—don't worry about it."

Jake drank his coffee. I would've drunk mine if there'd been any left. I couldn't believe that my own boyfriend hadn't noticed that he'd been hooking up with Rina for a week, when Jake, my freakin' lab partner, a guy I hadn't spoken to in years, had realized something was up right away. He didn't know what was wrong. But he knew that I hadn't been myself. I wanted so badly to tell him . . . everything. But who would believe my story?

"Sorry I ditched you freshman year," I said abruptly. Jake looked at me, surprised.

"Uh . . . okay, thanks," he said. "It's not that big a deal."

"No, it is," I said, sitting up in my chair. "It's totally a big deal, and I totally suck. Just because we weren't in the same classes anymore doesn't mean we should've stopped hanging out. I mean, I got busy with school and stuff, but I could've called. Or e-mailed. Or something."

"Yeah, me too," Jake agreed. He shrugged, half-smiling. "We both suck, I guess. We were kids though—what're you gonna do?"

I sat up straighter. "We used to hang out all the time. You've been here before. In this kitchen." I suddenly had a flashback to us as seventh-graders, toasting Pop-Tarts after school and then taking them down to the basement.

"Yeah, I know," Jake said, looking around. "You've still got that giant fork on the wall." He smiled at the decoratively carved wooden fork my mom put up years ago, when she'd received it and the accompanying giant wooden spoon (which had since fallen off the wall and broken, thanks to an accidental bump by me) as a gift.

"And I used to be at your house all the time too, although you moved, didn't you?" I asked.

"Yeah," he answered, "last year. Just a couple blocks over from our old house though."

"I heard about that. I don't know where I heard it—not from you because we weren't talking, but I guess . . ."

"It's a small school—word travels." Jake shrugged.

"True," I agreed.

We sat in silence again for a while.

"Anyway," I finally said, getting up to start some coffee now that both of our cups were empty. "Sorry if I've been acting strange. I've just been stressed out lately. You know."

"Oh, I know," he said. "Congrats on surviving your hell week, by the way. Did you get your application in on time?"

"Yeah," I nodded, trying to hide the anger in my voice as I replayed the image of Rina clicking the mouse for me.

"And the SATs went well?"

"Yeah, pretty well," I said, watching the water begin to boil on the stove. At least I'd done the SATs myself.

"Cool," Jake said. "Well, I'm sure you'll get into Yale. I've never seen anyone work as hard as you. So unless they're total idiots, which is possible, they've gotta let you in."

I smiled wistfully. *No*, I thought, *they'll be letting Rina in.*

"What's wrong?" Jake asked.

"Oh," I said. There he went, reading my mind again, or sort of, at any rate. "Nothing's wrong. Except . . ."

Huh.

". . . except that I might not want to go to Yale," I said. I turned and looked at him as if he'd just said something insane, instead of me.

Jake laughed a little. "What? Come on, that's like your lifelong dream."

"But I think . . . I think actually it isn't," I said, again staring as if he were the one spouting nonsense. "Yeah. No. It isn't."

I suddenly realized why I'd flown off the handle at Paul yesterday. He'd been talking about Yale like it was a foregone conclusion that we would go there together, whereas I . . .

I must've realized somewhere along the way that I didn't want it to be foregone. Yale was one option, but it sure as hell wasn't the only one.

Frankly, it didn't have to be one at all.

I almost giggled, thinking about how different high school would've been if I'd figured this out earlier.

How many times had I sucked up an extracurricular I didn't like, just to pad my résumé? How many times had I ditched out on something fun? If I went to Yale, it meant another four years of doing the same—four years of making myself miserable. I didn't want that. I didn't want to have worked this hard just to sentence myself to the same thing.

I mean, how glad was I that right now I was here, at home, instead of in New Haven, faking my way through a campus visit?

Very glad.

Ecstatic, actually.

I looked over at the stove. In the pot, the water was at a rolling boil. In fact, some of it had boiled away.

"Wow." Jake had been watching my face. His eyes looked a little amused and a lot impressed.

"Yeah," I agreed, turning off the stove. "I don't think Yale's for me." I suddenly didn't want coffee. I couldn't believe those words had just come out of my mouth. I'd said it out loud, and just like that, it was normal. Just like that, I wasn't going to Yale, and that was fine.

"You sure?" Jake asked.

"Yeah," I answered, nodding. "Yes."

"Well, cool," Jake said. "Now you're free to come to art school with me."

"What the hell would I do at art school?" I asked.

"Nude modeling," he answered instantly.

"Right, of course. What a stupid question."

"I know. Dummy."

We sat in silence again, sort of smiling at each other. Finally Jake got up. "I should get going." He gathered up his stuff. "Thanks for letting me crash your morning."

"Likewise," I said, following him toward the front door.

"No need to show me out—I've been here a million times," said Jake.

"True," I agreed. "Hell, we should probably go down in the basement and play video games or something, for old times' sake."

"I actually would have no problem with that," he answered, grinning and pausing for a split second to see if I was serious before opening the door. "Later." He hopped off the porch and started walking toward his car.

Wait.

Video games.

Which were like computer games.

Which included SimuLife.

I ran out the door, oblivious to the fact that I was now in the freezing cold in just my running pants and a T-shirt.

"Jake!" He rolled down his car window and stopped backing out of the driveway.

"What?"

"You don't happen to remember a game called Simu-Life, do you?"

Jake paused thoughtfully, and then smiled. "Yeah, actually. That game was so pointless. Although I kinda liked being a rock star–slash–bakery owner so I could get groupies and free cupcakes. And Bizarro You—if I recall correctly—wore a lot of body glitter?"

Oh my God.

"You don't happen to still have a disk for that, do you?" I asked. *Please have it. Please have it, please have it, please have it. . . .*

Jake winced. "Yeek, I doubt it. Although when we moved we just chucked everything in the new basement, so it might be buried in there somewhere."

"I could . . . really use that disk," I said, struggling to keep my voice from turning into an excited squeak.

"How come?" he asked.

How come indeed? I couldn't come up with a convincing lie—or even an unconvincing lie—so I went with the truth.

"Because the SimuLife version of me came out of the computer and I need to cancel my account and get rid of her," I deadpanned.

Jake laughed. "Well, you're welcome to come over and look for it," he said. "I'll help you—I'm just warning you that my basement is a sty. And I might've thrown it out."

"Yeah, if you don't mind, I'll come over," I said, shivering a little as I bounced from foot to foot, making little prints in the dusting of snow. "Um, is now good? I'm kind of gross from running, but—"

"Didn't even notice," Jake said. "Sure, now's good, but don't say I didn't warn you." He put his car in park and waited as I raced back into my house and threw on my coat. I took my hair down from its ponytail, finger-combed the waves, swiped some lip gloss on, and ran back out to the car.

We drove to his house in comfortable silence. I waved hi to his mom, who managed to muster a "Hello, Kate" as if the last time I'd seen her was days, not years, ago, on our way down to the basement.

"Wow. You meant it," I said, surveying the scene from the bottom of the staircase. Even in the dim lighting, I could see it was a nightmare.

"You're damn right I did," Jake answered, flipping a few switches. The rest of the lights came on, brightly illuminating the whole room, which was first of all gigantic, and second of all the messiest, most cluttered thing I'd ever seen. Boxes were piled floor to ceiling. A bunch of old furniture was in one corner. There were stacks of books, papers, old CD cases, board games, art supplies, and sports equipment everywhere, and the Ping-Pong table was littered with stuff as well. "Welcome to hell," Jake said cheerfully. "You got a while?"

"I have all day," I said. Hell, I had all night too, if that's what it took to find the disk.

"Well, let's get started."

Jake and I both grabbed boxes, practically choking on the thick clouds of dust as we started going through the stuff inside. The first few boxes yielded nothing but old clothes, so we moved them against the wall and kept going.

"So much for lucking out," Jake said.

"It's still *possible* . . ." I answered hopefully.

Yeah, well.

After an hour, Jake's dad came downstairs with trash bags and said that while we were at it, we might as well do them a favor and start chucking anything that clearly wasn't needed anymore. After three hours, his mom came downstairs with a pizza and a six-pack of Coke. After four hours, Jake was about to pass out from having been up for a day and half straight, despite all the Cokes and the sour gummi worms he was eating by the handful. But he'd finally stumbled on a group of three boxes labeled "computer games." We held our breath.

They contained books.

After five hours, we found actual computer games, in

a group of boxes labeled "Jake schoolwork." The first box also had a bunch of old photos, one of which I held up.

"Wow," I said innocently, showing Jake a picture of himself as a toddler. He was sporting a shiny black bowl cut and a pink apron over a striped shirt and corduroy pants, and he was holding a spatula.

"Wow yourself," Jake answered, picking up an old eighth-grade class photo, in which he looked more or less the same as he did now, whereas I was wearing head-to-toe pink, with my hair frizzed out in a triangle around my head. "Besides," he said, snatching his baby pic out of my hand, "you know you want a man who can cook."

"I actually want a man with a bowl cut," I said.

"Yeah, well, that can be arranged."

We kept on looking. It very much sucked. Jake fell asleep and I had to kick him awake. Then he fell asleep again and I threw a stuffed bear at his head. And then, suddenly, halfway through my search of a giant wooden toy chest, I screamed.

"Found it!" I was holding the SimuLife disk in my hands. "FOUND IT!" I impulsively hugged Jake, who was sitting back on his heels next to a box labeled "crap." He lost his balance and we tumbled over into a dusty pile of papers. We both sneezed, and a spider skittered out onto the floor next to my head. But I was far too happy to be particularly squicked. I just disentangled myself from Jake, stood up, and waved my arms around while my feet did a happy dance.

"Thank you!" I said to Jake. "Thank you thank you thank you!" I twirled in a circle, dramatically brandishing the disk.

"You're welcome," Jake said, amused. He got up and dusted off his hands. "So are you gonna tell me why you need that?" he asked.

"Yes, at some point," I said breathlessly, gathering my coat and my bag. "But you'll think I'm insane and right now I gotta go thank you bye!" I raced up his basement stairs, sprinted out the door, realized that I hadn't driven, then raced back up the sidewalk to his porch and rang the door-bell.

"Uh, can I get a ride home?" I asked sheepishly when Jake opened the door. He laughed and nodded and showed me the car keys he was already holding.

Fifteen minutes later, I was in my room in front of my computer. I took a deep breath, then stuck the SimuLife disk into the drive. The game booted up and started.

Yes.

"Welcome to SimuLife!" said the window. As annoying background music played and some rather cheap-looking graphics swirled around on-screen, I clicked on "options" and then went to "cancel account." I clicked it and held my breath. *Please let this work. Please.*

A window popped up. "Are you sure you want to cancel this account?" it asked. "Yes," I said out loud. "Hell to the Y-E-S." I moved the cursor over to the "yes" box. The arrow hovered over it, waiting for me to click.

But I didn't click it.

There was something else I had to do first.

CHAPTER TWENTY-TWO
TUESDAY, DECEMBER 18

THE YALE WEBSITE LISTED ITS ADMISSIONS office hours as nine to six. I called at nine on the dot. I stood by the window as I waited for someone to answer, gazing out into the bright, windy day. The bare tree branches in the yard were swaying, and a few leaves that our fall raking had missed skittered across the dead grass. Okay, it was more than just a few. My mom and I suck at raking.

Someone picked up the phone. "Admissions." It was a young-sounding, pleasant female voice.

"Hi," I said, then paused. Was I really going to do this? It felt like just a split second, but it was enough for the voice to go, "Hello? Hello?"

"Hi," I said again quickly. "My name is Katerina Larson, and I want to withdraw my application." There. I'd said it. And it felt surprisingly normal.

"What?" the voice asked.

"I just sent in my application and I was wondering if I could withdraw it," I repeated.

"I'm sorry, but we can't give refunds."

"That's fine," I said. "I don't need a refund. I just need to cancel my application."

There was a long pause. "Can you hold, please?"

"Yep," I said, but she'd already left. I listened to some weird hybrid of classical and electronic Muzak for a few seconds, and then another voice came on the phone. Equally female, equally pleasant, but much older-sounding.

"Hello?"

"Hi," I answered. I repeated my request, spelled my name when she asked me to, and gave her my address, phone number, and e-mail.

A keyboard clacked. "Are you sure?" asked the woman. "Have you talked to your parents about this?"

"Yes, I'm sure, and no, I haven't talked to them," I said. This was taking longer than I'd thought it would.

"But don't you want to wait and see if you're accepted first, and make your decision then?" she asked.

"Well, the thing is, I don't really know that I even want to go to college this fall, so . . ." That was the other wrinkle I'd figured out overnight. No Yale next year had turned into no anything (well, no college, at any rate). I'd been on the same path for too long, and it was time to get off of it. Way off.

"You know, you can always defer," said the woman. "If you get in you can just defer for a year. That way you'll still have the option."

"Yeah, I thought of that," I said patiently, "but I decided on this instead." I *had* thought about it, and my conclusion was that putting an official one-year limit on the freedom I was about to give myself was basically the same as not giving myself that freedom at all. It wasn't like I didn't have the option to reapply . . . and in a year, I probably would. But I also wanted the option not to. "So could you please just withdraw me?"

"All right," the woman said after a pause. "Let me just go into your file here." I waited for the Muzak, but she appeared to have just put the phone down. There was a sort of bonking noise, and then her keyboard clicked away in the background.

"Oh," she said, picking the phone back up. "It says here that you've checked in for your campus visit already. Did you not enjoy it?"

"Oh, no, it was great," I said, making my voice sound casual even as my stomach knotted. Rina was no doubt bopping all over New Haven right this second, checking out what she assumed would be her hometown for the next four years. "It has more to do with my issues right now, not the school."

"Ah, the old 'it's not you, it's me' excuse," the woman

said, sounding almost amused. "Okay, it's almost done."
And a few more clacks of the keys later, it was.

Goodbye, Yale.

I hung up, took a deep breath and texted Paul.
Starbucks run? I was on a roll of accomplishing big things
today—if one thing counted as a roll—and I wanted to
keep it going.

Sure, came his reply almost instantly.

A little while later, he met me in the parking lot. I'd
beaten him by several minutes and gotten us both coffees already. "Wanna take a walk?" I asked, offering him
a cup.

"It's freezing," he said, taking it from my hands and
bending to give me a quick kiss on the cheek.

"Hence the coffee," I said. "Come on, nature trail
behind the school?"

He raised an eyebrow, but followed me toward the
soccer fields anyway. My steps were quick. I was glad to be
on my feet and moving. I wanted space and distance all
around. Paul had been right though. It was indeed freezing
out. The sun was brighter than it had been earlier, but the
wind had picked up and we were both shivering. Neither
of us was wearing a hat, and I could see Paul's ears already
reddening.

"What's wrong?" asked Paul, as we crunched through
the dead leaves on the trail. I couldn't decide whether to

warm my hands on my coffee cup or keep them inside my coat sleeves and cradle the cup precariously. The wind was whipping my hair around my face, sticking it to my lip balm, and I couldn't reach up and unstick it. Bleh.

"I called Yale this morning," I said. "And withdrew my application."

Paul stopped walking. "What?" he asked.

"I withdrew my application from Yale," I repeated, stopping a few feet away from him. He stared at me some more, his eyes puzzled, and my stomach knotted a little, hoping he wouldn't start yelling.

But his face registered only shock and confusion, and after a long moment, he asked simply, "Why?"

I sighed and leaned back against a tree. "I just . . . I just don't think I would be happy there," I said, my voice shaking a tiny bit. "At least not now. Not this fall."

"But I'm gonna be there," Paul said.

"I know." I waited a moment. "But I won't."

From the look on his face, he knew exactly where this was going.

And that's exactly where it went.

I didn't have a speech prepared. I didn't know what I was going to say until the words were coming out of my mouth. All I knew was that I was telling the truth: that I hadn't felt like myself lately around him; that I didn't quite know what I wanted right now, but it wasn't the same thing

I'd been doing for the past three years; that I was somehow confused and sure at the same time, and that it all added up to me not going to Yale, to us not going there together, to us not being together anymore. Paul listened and occasionally nodded, and as I talked, I could see the resignation growing on his face. Resignation and acceptance. No anger, though. No defensiveness.

"Yeah," he repeated, as I rambled on. "Yeah. Yeah."

He looked sad. I felt sad. He didn't look heartbroken though, and that was all I needed to know that I'd done the right thing.

We were still standing on the nature trail, barely twenty feet from where it started. So much for taking a walk.

"So . . . what's gonna happen for the rest of the year?" Paul asked.

"I don't know," I said. It was true. I suddenly realized that now neither of us had a guaranteed prom date. It was months away, but that was the first thought that sprang to mind. Silly, but there it was—a reminder that what I'd just done had the huge consequences I'd thought about, and also little ones I hadn't. Everything I had planned, everything I'd thought was going to happen as I rode out the end of high school, was different now.

But that's the way I wanted it.

I stared into the trees in the distance for a while, hugging myself for warmth, and then glanced back at Paul. He looked thoughtful, and, for the first time in the entire time I'd known him, very, very tired.

"Do you want a ride home?" he asked.

"No, I'll take the bus," I said.

"You sure?"

"Yeah, I'm sure."

I was lying. I was going to walk.

My footsteps scratched on the cold, empty sidewalk as I bypassed the bus stop and started the long trudge home. I knew that Paul and I would talk again. After all, we ran in the same group of friends, and neither of us was the type to make things awkward. But still, it felt like an ending. We weren't getting back together—that I knew.

My phone beeped, and I stopped walking to dig it out of my bag. It was a text from Anne, which read, I have it on good authority that u and jake hooked up. Just want 2 let u know im gonna tell paul.

What?

My eyes widened and I slammed my phone shut, wondering how the hell she'd found out about Jake and Rina. Had someone overheard me and Jake talking in the hallway that day? Had she asked Jake himself, and he didn't bother to lie? I covered my eyes with my hand for a moment, then started walking again, briskly and blindly moving forward.

And suddenly it dawned on me that it didn't matter.

None of it mattered. Whatever she said, whatever she thought she knew, it wasn't the truth. And if Paul listened to her, and believed her over me, well . . . that wasn't my problem anymore.

I texted her back, **Do whatever u want. We broke up.** The phone didn't beep again.

It took me until late afternoon to get home, and I was surprised to see my mom sitting at the kitchen table when I walked in. My fingers and toes were well on their way to numb, and my cheeks and ears were bright red. But if I was surprised to see her, she was *stunned* to see me. She'd been drinking tea and going through the mail, and she choked on the former and dropped a bunch of the latter. Papers drifted to the floor as she sputtered and finally managed to say hi.

"Hi Mom," I answered.

"What are you doing here?" she asked, taking off her glasses and setting them on the table. "Why aren't you in New Haven?"

"Why aren't you in Kansas City?" I countered, taking off my coat and chucking it over the back of a chair. Her being home totally threw off my plan for the evening, which was to wallow in misery in front of the TV with as many sugary foodstuffs as I could find.

"The deal fell through," my mom said, tucking her hair behind her ears. "Very annoying, but this company's notorious for last-minute stuff like this. Back to you—why aren't you still at Yale?"

I sat down at the table across from her as she leaned over to pick up the mail she'd dropped. "I withdrew my application," I said. My voice was way calmer than it had been a few hours ago with Paul. Maybe practice made perfect.

My mom's eyes widened. "What? Why? Oh my God, is something wrong?"

"No, nothing's wrong," I said. "Seriously. I'm fine. I just . . . I just decided that I want to take a year off before starting college. You know? I've sort of spent the last four years doing exactly the same thing, I want to see if . . . I just want to do something different for a little bit."

"Like what?" she asked.

"Like . . . I don't know," I said. Not uncertainly, just matter-of-factly. "That's the whole thing. I just spent all of high school turning myself into some sort of getting-into-college machine. And if I go straight to college, I'm going to turn into some getting-into-grad-school machine. And I mean, is that it? Is that all I do? That's lame. And it's extra lame because I don't even enjoy it." I took a deep breath. "So now I want to do something else. Something that's actually me. And I don't know what it is yet, but I will. Because I've thought about it. I've thought about it a *lot* lately."

My mom looked at me, ever so slightly amused at my rambling, but also like she was truly paying attention.

"Hmm," she said, swirling her tea around in her mug. She took a slow sip, keeping her eyes on my face.

"Are you mad?" I asked. She didn't look mad, but maybe it was because she was so incredibly mad she'd gone full circle into looking normal again.

"No," she said. "I'm not mad. I just—are you sure this is what you want?"

"Yes." I nodded a quick, sharp nod.

"Are you sure you don't want to just defer for a year?"

"Mom, I had this exact conversation this morning with the woman in the admissions office. Yes. I'm sure." I stared right at her.

"What if you still go to Yale but then just skip class and party a lot?"

I burst out laughing. "Mom!"

"Okay," she said. "Just checking." She smiled a small smile and got up from the table.

Good lord, was that it? That was all the reaction my mom was going to have? I watched to see if she was hiding some sort of soon-to-be-explosive anger, but her face was serene. This was too good to be true; maybe she was in shock right now and the real wrath would rain down on me later?

"Does Paul know?" my mom asked. *Aha, here we go.*

"Paul and I broke up," I said. My voice, again, was surprisingly calm.

"Paul and you *what?*" My mom's mouth fell open, and suddenly all the astonishment from when I had first walked in was back in her face. "Oh, honey, I'm sorry!"

"It's okay," I said.

My mom sat back down at the table and stared at me. "Wait, did you guys break up and that's why you don't want to go to Yale? Because, honey, that's not—"

"No, no, it happened the other way around," I said hastily. I suddenly realized what it sounded like from her point of view and wanted to set her straight as quickly as possible. "The two things are totally unrelated. I mean, they are related, but they're not related. Not like that."

"Okay." My mom nodded, then got up to make me some tea. She was trying her best to look supportive and encouraging, but I could see tiny threads of concern beginning to creep into her face as she started thinking about all the implications of what I'd decided to do.

"And by the way," I added quickly, not wanting her to start panicking, "I'm not just going to, like, sit around the house all year or anything. I thought I would travel . . . or maybe get a job . . . but whatever I do, I'll have a whole itinerary and financial plan, okay? I'll map the whole thing out. So don't worry." I gave her my very best "everything's gonna be fine" face.

My mom smiled. "Oh, I'll worry, but I'm glad you've thought that far ahead, at least. My über-smart daughter."

She shook her head, then dunked a tea bag into a mug of hot water and handed it to me, along with a little squeeze-bottle of honey.

"Mostly book-smart," I said wryly. "Kind of another reason I need to skip out on school for a year. You know. So I can become hardened and streetwise and beat down by the system."

"Ha. Very funny, missy." My mom sat back down and passed me a spoon.

"Okay, well, maybe not the beat-down part. Or hardened. Streetwise I could probably use." I stirred honey into my tea and took a sip, then stirred in a bunch more.

"Probably." My mom smiled, and I felt happy, like actually, truly happy for the first time all day. Until the smile abruptly disappeared from her face.

"Kate?" she asked, staring at me. "If you're here, where's your car?"

Christ. Rina was still in New Haven with my car.

"I'll have it back by tomorrow," I told her.

"But where is it?" she repeated.

"Um . . ." I thought fast. "It was making a weird noise, so Paul told me to take it to his dad's car guy to have it looked at. I'll go get it tomorrow, don't worry."

My mom kept staring at me.

"Seriously. I'll have it back," I repeated.

"Okay," she said finally. I knew she didn't believe my

lie, but the look on her face told me that she wasn't going to push the issue. She did, however, scooch back in her chair and stand up. "So what does my non-college-bound daughter want for dinner?" she asked.

"Ice cream?" I answered hopefully. "Although I don't think we have any. . . ."

"Oh, we will," my mom said, patting me on the head. "We'll have all that your cute little face can stuff down." She got her coat, handed me mine, and we both got in her car to drive to the grocery store.

TO DO

- Whatever the hell I want from now on

(within reason)

(and the bounds of the law)

(okay I'm exaggerating, but I know what I mean)

(I should probably stop making these lists)

CHAPTER TWENTY-THREE

IT WAS NEARLY TEN O'CLOCK AT NIGHT. MY mom, zonked from her business trip and sugar crashed from our ice cream dinner, had gone to bed an hour ago, and I was sitting in my room at my computer, my calm from earlier in the day beginning to evaporate. I had an e-mail, a text, and a voice mail from Kyla, none of which I'd answered yet, in which she demanded to know what the hell had happened with me and Paul. I had similar e-mails from several other people as well, none of which I felt like dealing with. Mostly though, I was wondering what was up with Rina.

The garage door opened.

Well, there was my answer.

I winced at the noise and prayed that the sound didn't wake my mom up. Rina apparently had no such worry, as she pounded up the staircase and threw open the door of my room, a triumphant smile on her face. I instantly put my finger to my mouth, shushing her before she could say anything.

"Mom's asleep," I hissed. "She came back from her business trip early, so be quiet, will you? Didn't you see her car in the garage?"

Rina ignored me and instead dropped all her (well, my) belongings in the middle of the floor. "I kicked so much ass on that interview!" she whisper-screamed. "They loved me, like I knew they would. I'm in. I just *know* it!"

"Congratulations," I said cheerfully. "That's great. But I withdrew my application."

Rina stared at me. "What?" she asked. "*WHAT*?!" She searched my eyes and realized that I wasn't kidding, and her face began to contort with rage. I suddenly knew what it was like to have been her the day I stormed in and found her making out with Paul. I could feel her murderous gaze like actual knives on my skin.

"What did you just say?" she repeated.

"You heard me," I answered coolly. I gave Rina the same evil smile she'd given me a few days ago, and I watched as she registered it and reacted the exact same way I had—with horror and anger and shock. "Sorry," I continued. "I won't be going to Yale. Looks like you won't be either. And by the way?" I jerked my head toward my computer monitor.

Rina followed my gaze. "What, did you write another earnest-but-lame essay?" she asked, walking toward me. She stopped dead a few feet away, her eyes growing wide as she saw what was on the screen.

"No," I answered calmly. I nodded toward the "Welcome Back to SimuLife," notice shining brightly into Rina's eyes. "And if I were you, I wouldn't make any sudden movements." My hand held the mouse cursor directly over the "cancel account" button, and I gave her a cold, condescending smile. *One click of this and you can rot in hell*, I thought. Rina visibly stopped breathing for a moment, and then her shoulders sagged. She slowly turned around and sat down on my bed.

"You found the disk," she whispered, all the fight draining out of her voice.

I nodded.

"I guess this is it then, huh?" she said.

"Pretty much," I agreed matter-of-factly. For the first time, I felt totally in control. Probably because, thanks to Jake's SimuLife disk, I was. And because I was in control, I wasn't mad at Rina anymore. What was the point? She'd be gone soon anyway.

Rina seemed to know all of this. Her face was ashen, and even though she was dressed in my jeans and a black sweater, she suddenly looked like the girl who'd shown up two weeks ago in glitter and pastel pink.

"Come over here and look at the computer," I said.

"No," Rina answered. "Just do what you have to do." She lay down like a corpse, her head on my pillow, and closed her eyes.

"I did," I said. "That's why I withdrew my application."

Rina didn't move.

"I get what you were trying to do," I continued. "Seriously. I know you just wanted to have fun, and I know your life in the game was really boring. And I know that was my fault—I should've made it more interesting for you." I paused for a moment. "So I did."

Rina opened her eyes, still lying down, and slowly turned her head to look at me.

"We can't keep you out here because you belong in there," I said, tilting my head toward the computer. "But I think you might like it better now."

Rina stared at me wide-eyed, but still didn't move.

"Come on," I said. "Seriously, you need to look." I took the cursor off "cancel" and started navigating around my SimuLife account. Rina tentatively got up to look over my shoulder. Her eyes widened.

"You fixed my house," she said, staring at the screen in shock.

"Yep," I said. I moved the mouse, showing her around her new house. The outside was the same as it had been, but inside it was totally redone. "I did some interior decorating," I said, pointing and clicking at various rooms. Each one was now painted a different color, instead of the game's default shades of beige and white, and there was all new furniture. In the basement, there was a huge flat-screen TV, and I'd put one in the living room as well.

"Are those HD?" Rina asked hesitantly.

"Yep," I answered. "HD with DVR, both of them."

"Wow," she said quietly. "Thanks." She leaned in closer to the monitor, so far forward that she was practically draped over me, and I stood up and moved out of the way. "Here," I said, handing her the mouse. "Check it out for yourself."

Rina looked at me gratefully and sat down in my computer chair, then started navigating around her house. She clicked here and there, gasping a little when she saw the multiple bookshelves that were now filled with books, and practically dropping her jaw to the ground when she saw that I'd redone her bedroom to look exactly like mine. It was a perfect, computerized replica, from the walk-in closet (which I'd filled with clothes, a lot of them like stuff I owned, but also a bunch of Hot Topic-y stuff, and of course a ton of pink for good measure) to the big round mirror over the dresser to the computer desk in the corner—the one she was sitting at right now.

"I also got you a car," I said, pointing at the garage.

Rina clicked on it and squeaked with approval when she saw the little blue Honda Civic, just like mine, parked inside.

"But am I going to be all alone in there?" she asked, looking up at me. Her voice still sounded guarded, but there was a hint of excitement growing on her face.

"Hardly," I said, smiling a little. "I got you accepted into SimuLife University. You're a double major in journalism and poli-sci, but I can change that if you want."

"No, that's good," Rina said. Now she looked officially excited. "Where's . . . where's campus?"

I reached over, took the mouse for a moment, and showed her. "That's your dorm," I said, pointing the arrow at a modern-looking building surrounded by trees. "I scored you a single so you don't have to room with anybody, but the hallway's got like twenty other rooms on it, so you'll meet lots of people. And that's Parker. He's your freshman orientation leader." I watched as Rina moved the mouse over Parker, a computerized hottie standing in the dorm's courtyard; he was tall and brown-haired like Paul, but with green eyes instead of blue, and just a wee bit more buff.

Rina smiled. "Niiiice."

"I figured," I answered, smiling back at her.

"You gave him a good personality though, right?" she asked.

"No, he's just a low-IQ piece of ass." I shoved her playfully with my elbow. "Of course I did, what do you take me for?"

Rina smiled and moused around the screen some more, checking out the classroom buildings, the students walking around campus in their "S.U." shirts, the college library, the gym, and a few of the other dorms. "You thought of everything," she said, shaking her head. Then suddenly her face broke into a huge grin. "Oh my God, you did think of everything!" She squealed as she clicked back onto her house and saw the outdoor hot tub in the backyard, next to some cute wicker patio furniture and a shiny red grill. There were Christmas lights strung on the hedges, and the whole thing was shaded by a huge pink and white striped umbrella.

"Well, you certainly did while you were here," I told her. "So I figured I owed you." Her backyard contained a giant trampoline now as well, since I remembered wanting one in middle school and my mom being too afraid of lawsuits to oblige.

Rina smiled at the sight of the trampoline, and then her face became serious. "I don't know if you owe me after what I did to you and Paul . . ." she said. She got up from the computer and sat down on the bed.

I paused for a second, then sat down next to her and took a deep breath. "No, I do owe you," I said. "You were right, you know. I wouldn't have made it through the past week without your help. So . . . thanks. For everything."

Rina turned to look at me. "You're welcome. And thank *you*. For everything." She looked around my room, then tilted her head toward my computer, indicating the SimuLife screen.

"No problem," I said.

"And I'm sorry I was such a whore."

I laughed. "Forgiven."

Rina laughed too, then held out a hand for me to shake. "I'll miss you!" she said cheerfully. "Even though hopefully Parker and his abs will be a nice distraction."

I grinned and gave her a quick hug. "Yeah, they will," I said. "And I'll miss you too."

Rina stood up and stretched, and I walked back to my computer and poised my hand over the mouse. "So . . . you ready?" I asked.

"Yeah," she answered, taking off the earrings she was wearing—my earrings—and setting them on the dresser. "Are you?"

"I'm actually not sure," I said, "but I kind of have to do it anyway."

"Yeah, I know." Rina smiled, turned, and walked into the closet. She waved goodbye over her shoulder and then closed the door.

I looked at my computer screen, went back to the

SimuLife main menu, moved the mouse over to "uninstall," and clicked it.

"Are you sure you want to uninstall SimuLife?" asked the popup window. I moved the mouse to the "yes" button and clicked. The computer whirred for a bit as a gray bar appeared on the screen, and then, from left to right, slowly turned blue.

"SimuLife successfully uninstalled," said the message on my computer.

I sat back, staring at the screen for a second, and then looked over at the closet again. "Rina?" I asked tentatively.

Nothing.

I got up, went over to the closet door, grabbed the knob, and took a deep breath. I opened the door and looked inside.

The closet was empty.

Well. That was that.

I collapsed facedown on my bed, almost shaking with relief. Rina was gone. Well, she wasn't gone—she was hopefully partying it up in her sweet new house and her sweet new dorm somewhere, with her sweet new boyfriend—but she was gone from my world. Finally. My life was my own again—and now that I was living it the way I wanted to, rather than the way I thought I had to, it felt more my own than ever.

Heh. That was either a pretty deep thought for a

seventeen-year-old kid, or just an incredibly pompous one. I mentally congratulated myself—at this point, either one was fine with me—then flipped over onto my back and stared at the ceiling. I breathed a long, full-body sigh.

My computer beeped.

Oh no.

I was too scared to look, then too scared not to. I got up and walked over to the computer. A little window had popped up . . . but, thank God, it was just an IM.

From Jake.

Hey, the message said. **What's up? Everything work out okay with that game disk?**

I smiled and sat down at the keyboard. **Yep,** I typed back. **Thanks.**

There was a pause, then Jake started typing again. **By the way, I heard about you and Paul. Are you okay? Do you want to talk about it?**

Yeah, I typed. **I mean no. I mean, thanks for asking, but yeah, I'm okay.** That was the truth, actually. I didn't want to talk about it, not because it was bothering me, but because it wasn't. I was happy Jake had asked, but I hadn't been thinking about it until he did.

Good, I'm glad, he typed. There was another long pause. **So . . . you wanna play SimuLife?** ☺

I laughed. **Oh God no,** I typed back. **It's a long story, but nooooo way.**

My cell phone rang and I picked it up. "What's the story?" Jake asked.

"You do not want to know," I answered, flopping down stomach-first onto my bed, and then turning over and leaning back against the pillows.

"Try me," he said.

"I might," I teased. *Oh, what the hell.* "Can I come over there?"

"Uh, sure." Jake sounded a tiny bit surprised. But he quickly recovered, and then added jokingly, "Why, you want a replay of last week in your living room?"

I laughed. "Well, that wasn't really me that day . . ." I started.

"Yeah, you said that before."

"But it should've been."

There was a long, long silence, and finally, Jake asked, "Seriously?"

"We've got a lot to talk about," I told him.

"Yeah," he agreed, his voice quiet and thoughtful. "I guess we do."

"Well, that'll be one of the discussion topics when I come over, then," I said, my voice cheerful now instead of pensive. "But first let's play a bunch of video games." I got up to grab my car keys.

Jake laughed. "Sure. What're you thinking, Halo? Call of Duty? BioShock? Gears of War?"

"Yikes, I don't know about the first-person shooters," I said, heading down the stairs to put on my coat. "I'm a little out of practice."

"Mario Kart? Guitar Hero? Rock Band? Wii Tennis?" Jake paused for a long beat. "Checkers?"

I laughed. "We'll figure it out when I get there," I said, opening the door to the garage. "I'm on my way."

"Cool," Jake said. "Can't wait."

Neither could I.

ACKNOWLEDGMENTS

Many thanks to Josh Bank, Allison Heiny, Bob Levy, Les Morgenstein, Nora Pelizzari, Sara Shandler, Andrea C. Uva, Farrin Jacobs, Gretchen Hirsch, Melissa Dittmar Bruno, everyone at Alloy Entertainment and HarperTeen, David Boxerbaum, Helena Heyman, Richard Abate, Greg Hodes, Adriana Alberghetti, and WME Entertainment.